Reflection in Glass

By Robin Densmore Fuson

Copyright Robin Densmore Fuson 2018
Forget Me Not Romances, a division of Winged Publications

All rights reserved. No part of this publication may be reproduced, stored in a retrieval system, or transmitted in any form or by any means, with the exception of brief quotations in printed reviews.

This book is a work of fiction. The characters in this story are the product of the author's imagination and are completely fictitious.

All rights reserved.

ISBN-13: 9781719822152

Now faith is the substance of things hoped for,
the evidence of things not seen.
Hebrews 11:1 KJV

Chapter One

Province of Maryland
1775

"Prudence, will you give me the honor of becoming my wife?"

Prudence gasped and placed her hand on her throat as Oliver knelt before her.

She flew to his arms with an outcry. "Yes!"

This outburst and demonstration of affection would have given her Aunt Emeline apoplexy. The young couple was completely alone, against propriety, but they were outdoors, after all.

Earlier, her aunt took to bed with a terrible headache and her parents were out. Granny would be dozing in her chair by the window but wouldn't be able to see them from her vantage point, had she opened her eyes.

Oliver picked her up and swung her in a circle. "That's my girl." He set her on her feet and held her at arm's length. She gazed up into his smiling face as the tears of joy clouded her eyes. Prudence blinked rapidly but the flow was relentless. Oliver released her and she took out her lace handkerchief to dab at the dribble. His grin continued and soon she got control of her tears and joined him in a dazzling smile.

"Shall we sit?" Oliver escorted her to the stone bench. They sat among a variety of roses, which bloomed in red, pink, yellow, and white, carrying a heady scent. "I already asked your father. He gave me his blessing. You had no idea?"

She shook her head. "Father didn't say a word. Nor did Mother. Had they known you decided to come today, they would not have left us alone. I'm sure Auntie and Granny are unaware, or the excitement of the event could not be kept silent."

"I ordered a set of gimmal rings to be made, one for each of us and the third, my brother will provide at our wedding. This will complete our set at the speaking of our vows."

Prudence clasped her hands together. "I can't wait to see them. When will they be ready?"

"I hope soon. First, I need to measure your finger." He slipped his hand over hers. "Your fingers are so delicate, yet long, slender, and strong and I want the rings to fit perfectly so they don't slip off."

Prudence watched him lift her hand to his mouth. The tender kiss felt like a butterfly. A chill ran up her arm. Normally, she would have donned silk, or at the very least linen gloves in his company, but his unexpected visit caught her unsuitably dressed. In the excitement, she had neglected to pull them on. She rather liked his touch on her skin.

"When shall we set the date?"

"We can talk to my parents tonight but it may get a bit tricky. Of course, I want to marry soon, but you know Mother. She will want a long engagement for propriety and to put together my wedding garments. Father will agree. I'm their only child and a daughter to boot. A disagreement shall erupt unless I sway her into my way of thinking." Prudence bit her lip. "I've always wanted a large wedding. Are you terribly disappointed?"

"Ah." He nodded. "I didn't know you would need so much time to prepare but I want you to enjoy a huge wedding. Shall we wed this next Christmas?"

"I'll see if I can talk Mother into it. If not, can we make it a spring wedding?"

"Early spring, say March or April?"

They sat in companionable silence for a moment. Oliver asked, "May I kiss you? After all, we are officially betrothed."

Prudence felt the heat rise up her cheeks. "Yes."

The tender kiss lasted a brief time. Too brief. She wanted another and another. She inwardly chided herself for these wanton feelings. Her minister father would be disappointed in her. Her mother might send her to her room, even though she had turned eighteen, and Aunt Emeline would no doubt swoon. She wanted to giggle at the supposed scene she'd cause.

The sound from the front announced the arrival of her parents. *Might he sneak another?* She raised her face and was rewarded.

She grinned. He winked at her as he stood and moved away four paces.

Prudence gazed around the table at her loved ones as they all tried to talk at once. Excitement of the upcoming nuptials rushed through the room like a zephyr. She smiled. They were intoxicated by the thoughts and plans as if they had drunk a dark brew. Oliver met her eyes and lifted an eyebrow.

She held in a giggle as she raised her water glass to her lips. What must he be thinking? Did he love her enough to step into this crazy family? As if reading her mind, he nodded. She breathed deeply and exhaled, letting the tension fall away. They had always been friends who loved each other. He was already part of her life and family.

His family's plantation bordered hers to the north, but with a combined 1600 acres, one did not walk, one rode a horse or drove a buggy, to call. Since long before her birth each plantation had grown tobacco, but the prices had plummeted a while back and the fields now produced wheat, corn, a variety of vegetables, and had parcels for grazing cattle. His father also produced incredible horses—muscle bound and fast as lightning. His steed munched on hay in the barn and stood three hands taller than her gelding.

Laughter interrupted her musings. She found all

eyes on her. "What, pray tell, is so amusing?"

"The silly look on your face." Aunt Emeline smirked.

Prudence knew her aunt loved her and didn't take offense. "I was thinking of our plantation. Father, do you suppose we should try our hand at cotton?"

"Dear, what gave you that idea? The southern colonies grow that particular crop well. We made our transition and are quite satisfied with the profits. My father, and his, prided themselves in the green fields of tobacco and we now grow corn and wheat. Those white blossoms of cotton are just not the same."

She shrugged. "I only speculated, dear Father."

"Extra hands would be needed to pick and additional sleeping and cooking buildings to be built. A few dozen more slaves. I believe we do well to keep what we know works. Don't you agree, Oliver?"

Oliver winked at her before turning to her father. "Sir, in my humble opinion, new ideas are always welcome. A keen mind to go with a beautiful face is a blessing. Our land as well is producing a bumper crop, but I'm always open to discussion and investigation. They may lead to an even brighter future."

Prudence smiled as her heart soared. Oliver seemed to say the right thing, to take her side, and yet not offend her parents. A diplomat to say the least. She was a blessed woman indeed.

As the dessert dishes were taken away, the conversation drifted to the date of the wedding.

Mother said, "We need much more time to put on a decent wedding. I assume you want the spring thaw to be over so mud will not interfere with the buggy wheels and create havoc with your gown and satin slippers. I propose a June wedding."

"I love the snow and cold, how about January or February?" Prudence asked.

"Too soon."

Her father said, "Beulah, we should compromise. This is her wedding after all."

"Yes, dear." Her mother looked through the window for a moment while drumming her fingers on the table. "How about early May? or I suppose April would be a fine time."

"April it is! Oliver, is that a good time for you?"

His eyes held hers. "I cast my vote for tomorrow." He turned toward her parents. "But April is a pretty month. Spring it is."

Prudence smiled to herself. She had won a round without causing a scene and Mother thought it her idea.

"Hoofbeats. Someone is approaching at a gallop." Oliver stood.

Her father wiped his mouth on his napkin and rose at the sound of swift footfalls up the front porch steps. Oliver and her father rushed to the dining room's double doors. Oliver took hold of one knob and her father the other. The front door banged open and stomps could be heard on the hardwood floor approaching their location.

Prudence ran around the table to stand beside Mother, Auntie, and Granny. Her father nodded to

Oliver and in one accord, they opened the double doors. The intruder sprawled onto the floor. Her father placed his foot onto the man's back. "Move a muscle and I'll let my future son-in-law run you through." At that moment Silas, their butler, handed Oliver a saber. To make their point, Oliver let the man feel the tip of the saber. His other hand held a dagger.

Prudence knew he carried an extra strapped to his calf but had not seen him retrieve the deadly looking thing.

"Now Mr. Cox, you may rise slowly and state your business in a gentlemanly manner and remember, we have ladies present." Her father said.

Their neighbor rose at a much calmer pace than he had entered. Her father pulled over a chair. "Sit."

He dropped into the chair. "Your cattle have roamed into my fields. I swear, I'll shoot one and have him to feed my family come winter."

"See how easy it is to speak in a proper manner?" He turned. "Silas, please send Boon and a passel of men to catch the animals and right the fence."

"Yes sir." He nodded and left.

"Would you like some coffee, Mr. Cox?" Prudence's mother asked.

He glanced her way. "No thank you."

"I'm sorry there isn't any pie. Had you come calling earlier, you might have enjoyed some nice cherry."

Prudence clamped her lips tight to contain the grin.

Her father said, "You may take your leave.

Unless there is something else on your mind?"

Mr. Cox shook his head.

"Be aware, we will not tolerate an entrance in that manner again. With all the unrest in the colonies you're lucky we didn't shoot and ask questions after. Am I clear? You can knock and let Silas answer just like everyone else. My men do my bidding and better not be molested in any way."

Mr. Cox stood and turned to Oliver. "Future son-in-law. Humph." He took hold of the tip of the saber and moved it out of his way and proceeded out the door.

No one moved until the sound of horse hooves died out.

"What did he think would happen?" Auntie asked.

"Why didn't you run him through?" asked Granny.

Prudence said, "Oh Granny, I love you." She kissed the wrinkled cheek.

"I suggest we load up on arms and put them in strategic places around the house. His actions today cemented what I've been thinking."

"Where do his loyalties lie?" asked Oliver.

"He's loyal to the crown, I'm afraid. He may become a real threat. Ladies, it is time again to sharpen your marksmanship skills." He held up his hand. "Mother, I know you can shoot a bug off the oak across the river but everyone should practice."

Prudence lifted her eyebrow. *This should be entertaining.*

Chapter 2

Oliver eased into the saddle on Whistlejacket for the ride home. As Whistlejacket maneuvered the terrain, Oliver thought through the afternoon's visit. Prudence thrilled him. A beautiful, intelligent, and strong woman who completed him. His love for her grew as he had turned into a man.

At twenty-three years of age, and second in line to inherit the family estate, he felt confident his future also held the exquisite Prudence Ainsworth. Her family accepted him and he knew she returned the unique love he had for her. Children grown into lovers.

April was a long way off, nine months to be exact. Time changed people and situations. Their family structure or economy might shift. A horrible storm or drought, perhaps. The unrest with the British could escalate into a war. God forbid.

These brooding thoughts were not like him. He

shook his head. Must be something he ate.

Arriving home, Oliver unsaddled Whistlejacket and brushed him down before turning him over to the groom. The house only had a few lights glowing. Oliver detected light in his brother's and parent's rooms. He walked to the front where a hall candle lit the entrance hall. He lifted the candle and ignited the one next to it to carry to his chambers.

On the way, he knocked on his brother's door.

"Come."

He opened the well-oiled hinged door, creating only a whisper. "Jonas, she accepted my proposal! We will be married next April."

"You are one lucky man."

Oliver grinned. "I am indeed. Do you know anything about the Cox fellow south of the Ainsworth's?"

"Other than he is a loyalist and creates ruckus? He doesn't circulate with many friends and drinks himself under the table, I've been told. A real loud mouth. Why?"

"He barged into the household this evening. Granny said I should have run him through." He chuckled.

"Sounds like the old gal. I pray it doesn't come to that. What was he hot about?'

"He claimed Samuel's cattle got into his fields." He shook his head. "Samuel will make it right. As we all know, Samuel is honest and fair. You should have seen him. He was right angry but held the fire in. Only his eyes betrayed him. Steady as a massive oak tree and calm as an August night. I hope he got his point across to the wild Cox."

Jonas shrugged. "Good night, little brother."

"Good night." He closed the door and headed to his room.

Things were changing. He sensed it. Again, the brooding like a cloud descended upon him and the air carried a rustle of unrest. Things were brewing and he perceived they would bring life and death changes. This sixth sense came to him on many occasions in his lifetime. The first premonition he remembered distinctly. His father and uncle had gone into the French and Indian War which had lasted seven long years. At the end of the conflict— Oliver a mere ten years of age—had known in his gut they were on the road home. He sat at the window and waited. No one could dissuade him from his vigil and to everyone's surprise, they arrived later that day.

Other smaller intuitions occurred where he had been correct. This time, this intense feeling frightened him more than any other. What did the horizon hold that would come cascading into their line of sight? He shuddered.

Chapter 3

Christmas had come and gone. To Prudence, the frenzied activity made the special occasion seem like a blur. Normally, this time of year held long lazy days of making gifts and goodies but recent events outside their little world encroached and brought with it unrest. What did the future hold?

The wedding plans were well underway. The world thawed from winter and the start of the New Year screamed change. Good or bad, only the Lord of Providence knew.

Last August, Oliver came bearing the ring signifying their betrothal. A gloriously beautiful slim band with an etched vine carrying a few leaves and a notched out portion. "Let me place this on your finger."

She tugged off her glove and he slid it on her finger. The ring fit loosely but she thought it wouldn't fall off. She shook her hand to check. The ring stayed in place.

"Now, try it with your gloved hand."

The ring fit perfectly and she grinned up into his deep brown eyes. "It's beautiful. Thank you."

"I have one." He pulled it out and showed her the ring. "They fit together with the third that you will receive on our wedding day."

"Oh, Oliver! What a wonderful idea. We will be united like these rings."

Remembering that moment made all the tedious sewing seem worth it. Pearl buttons, a needle and thread, and coffee provided Prudence entertainment these past few hours as well as conversing with the other women in her family. Granny sat next to the window for the best light and embroidered new handkerchiefs. Across the room, Aunt Emeline scrutinized her own handiwork.

"Aunt Emeline, how are you coming with the new pocket pouch?"

"Mighty fine. I added silk inside for added thickness and comfort when you slide your hand inside. I made the ribbon a bit longer than the one you are wearing. You can adjust the pouch by making the bow smaller or larger."

"How very thoughtful of you."

Prudence turned toward her mother to survey the new undergarments that were folded in a pile next to her. Her mother had just finished those and now she attended to the last of the caps. A proper woman would need at least three caps. Two for everyday wear, a bit puffier and large enough for all her hair to be tucked underneath while she worked around the house. A larger ruffle for the brim to protect her if she ventured outdoors. To go calling, she needed a smaller fancier cap to sit atop her head. She preferred to let her hair be the natural brown God gave her, rather than the cultural use of grease and powder. But on occasions, she swayed to current fashion and did a proper job, using a citrus scent.

Also, she had new dresses, an extravagance her mother insisted on giving her, safely tucked upstairs in her wardrobe. Silk taffeta gowns with matching petticoats—one in a lovely yellow gold, another in a soft blue, and the third in a dusty rose. She felt spoiled indeed. These, along with her other clothes, would be quite sufficient for her new life.

Only a month away and she would be married and living at the Duke estate with her new husband. A smile spread as she remembered the sweet kisses they had secretly enjoyed.

Granny interrupted her thoughts. "Emeline and I went to Gibson's General Store to bring in our eggs and pick up more thread. Mr. Gibson nailed place cards to the walls with quotes from John Locke. If I remember correctly, 'I have no reason to suppose that he, who would take away my liberty, would not when he had me in his Power, to take away everything else.' Emeline, what was the one about shoes?"

"Oh that one. Let me think. Oh yes, 'Our incomes are like our shoes; if too small, they gall and pinch us; but if too large, they cause us to stumble and to trip.'"

"'Revolt is the right of the people.' Did you see that one, Mother?"

Granny nodded. "I believe that man is stirring up more trouble than any of us wants."

"Granny, are you referring to Locke or Mr. Gibson?" Prudence asked.

"Both, I reckon. Times are changing and I'm afraid we won't like the road we tread before we discover the outcome. There are two sides to every argument and those are coming more frequent. Britain has an iron fist and trying to pry the fingers open will either break them off or fling us into oblivion. Merciful Lord!"

A knock sounded on the door. Prudence rushed to answer. Her father stood with a variety of weapons in his arms. Boon stood next to him bearing another similar load. "Goodness, what is the matter? Are we under attack?"

Her father laughed. "Time for more practice and we will map out places for these to be available if a need arises. Come on, ladies, while the light holds. Gather your wraps and join us in the side yard."

Prudence turned back into the room. "You heard him. Mother, he's grinning like a school boy on his first big game shoot. What has become of my mild mannered pa? Boon too!"

Her mother rose and hugged her. "Adventure. The unknown. Preparation for his family. And, I'm afraid, he is masking his unease. He feels he may be away when trouble comes to us. He is responsible for my mother, sister, and you, our precious daughter."

The ladies went to the entry hall and grabbed their shawls before following the men out to the yard.

Flintlock musket in hand, Prudence reloaded as quickly as possible as her aunt and grandma did the same, having fired a few seconds ago. Her mother's musket fired and the acrid smell reached her nose as she took aim and did the same. She swung the rifle lower to start the process again as a shot sounded from Aunt Emeline's musket.

Her father called, "Halt! Good job, ladies. Please attach the bayonets and practice lunging."

Three white oak branches held stuffed sacks resembling persons. Prudence took a steady stance and proceeded to lunge her bayonet tipped flintlock into the defenseless sack. Again and again. Her arms ached from hoisting the fourteen-pound metal weapon for the last hour, first shooting and loading, and now attacking the fake enemy.

Her arms rebelled and she could well imagine her older counterparts were in deeper distress. Neither Granny nor Auntie complained as drops of sweat pooled into the band of their caps. Aunt Emeline lunged and the bayonet got caught. She must have expected it to release and lost her footing, causing her to stumble. The bag ripped, expelling the corn husks all over the downed woman. Auntie shrieked.

Prudence's mother and granny dropped their weapons and rushed to her as her father lifted her aunt out of the mess. Prudence waited and watched.

"Well, I never!" Aunt Emeline sputtered and pulled husks out of her mouth. Mother swiped at them from her clothes.

Pent up laughter exploded from Prudence.

Over-tiredness made her giddy.

The others glanced over as she leaned against the tree in unbridled giggles.

Oliver arrived on the scene and instantly realized what had transpired. He dismounted from Whistlejacket and draped the reins on a nearby bush.

Amused, he approached Prudence. "Did you ambush her?"

Prudence straightened. "No. Although that would've been a great idea. Father's training exhausted us and poor Auntie got her bayonet stuck and…" The giggles erupted again.

Oliver grinned. "After a while, I hope your dear auntie sees the humor in this situation. You might want to come for a stroll with me whilst your family helps her into the house and Boon cleans up the mess."

She nodded and accepted his arm.

He waited until she had cleared her throat and swiped at the tears caused from the laughter. "My sweet Prudence, I need to tell you something that may make you a bit upset."

He felt her stiffen. "Go ahead."

"As you are too aware, times are shifting and men are gearing up to stand against Britain even more so than what has already transpired. Men in our county as well as others all over Maryland Province are putting together training regiments of sorts. We want to be prepared to do what is necessary to protect our way of life."

"You said 'we.'"

"Yes. I signed a letter stating my cooperation. Tempers are flaring, first in Boston, then in Annapolis, and more recently in Chestertown—what they are referring to as tea parties with tea now in the bay and ships burning. I agree with the words written by First Citizen in the Gazette, 'Igniting men's continence's and honor to stand against tyranny, we must be prepared.' My training starts in two days and in a fortnight we will meet up with other counties."

"My goodness. So soon. I know you, my beloved, and I assumed you would not sit by as these incidences accelerated. My father talks of nothing else these days even in the pulpit. I'm afraid he will join forces too. He heightened our awareness of an immediate disaster by drilling us to a near faint."

"He, as I do, want you ladies safe. No better way, than being well trained. He and I have spoken and I commend his diligence on your training. We will have to leave you ladies to fend for yourselves, I'm afraid."

"We will be married, shan't we?"

"My dear Prudence, that is my strongest heart's desire. Can you talk some sense into your mother and we wed tonight or tomorrow?"

Chapter 4

Oliver said, "Sir, please explain your reasoning."

Mr. Ainsworth, Oliver's future father-in-law said, "Have a seat and we'll discuss the matter."

Oliver sat in the chair adjacent to the desk. Mr. Ainsworth took the other. "You will be my son-in-law, Lord willing, but later, when all this has blown over. Sadly, we are about to embark in a war. I don't want my only child married and widowed the same year." He held up his hand. "I am not saying that will happen, but it might. War is fickle as to who comes out in one piece.

"Prudence loves you and will wait indefinitely for you. I have seen and heard of too many woman with child from the wedding night. War is brutal to all and our women are left here to take care of land and each other and don't need the burden of a newborn. As a man of honor, I ask you to honor my request and not wed before you march out of the county."

Oliver sat in stunned silence. He hadn't expected this. His mind and heart reeled. His beloved Prudence stood her ground with her mother, who relented and gave her consent for the couple to be married tomorrow but now... What should he do? He loved her. Desired her as his wife. But. Yes, leaving her a widow with child, in foresight, a man of honor would never do. Would that happen? Only the good Lord knew. Would she understand or would her love turn sour from the postponement? *Oh Lord! Give me wisdom! Help me be worthy of my love for her and put her wellbeing before mine. I yearn for her. I am only a man. Give me the willpower needed to explain and keep my word.*

Oliver, deep in anguished thought, did not realize he had been left alone. His hand wiped the perspiration from his brow and the tears that had formed in his tightly closed eyes. He took a steadying breath and rose. He understood what he must do. He asked for strength and the right words as he went in search of his lovely Prudence. *His. Not yet*, but Lord willing.

Oliver found her in the parlor. Mysteriously, he didn't encounter any family or staff member on his quest. She sat by the window. Light spilled on her chestnut locks making them glow with a golden hue. His eyes traveled to her pearl white skin and perky nose. Ruby lips caught his attention. A burning desire to capture them with his own almost made his heart stop. Why didn't he scoop her up and carry her away with him? Away from the madness of this world? Time. He needed time. But there was no time.

She smiled. A radiant smile he burned into his memory.

She rose. "Oliver, Mother has agreed. We can be married tomorrow!" She started toward him but stopped. "What's wrong?"

He took a quick step into the room and gathered her to himself. She gasped.

He rested his chin on her head. "I'm sorry to be so direct but I wanted to hold you before we talk." He reluctantly released her, took her hand, and led her to the settee. "I'm afraid, my cherished Prudence, we need to wait until this unrest is over before we give our pledge. I love you and want our time together to be slow and long. A sweet marriage built on time and trust. We need to build our relationship eye to eye. I can't honor you with my presence as a husband should, if I am in a scrimmage far away in another colony."

Her eyes widened. "What are you saying? Don't you want me?"

"Oh, my darling, yes I want you! I desire you, to have and to hold, for better or for worse. You are my life and I wish to make you my wife. But I want to keep my vows of a lasting love. I don't intend to frighten you but war may break out and I could be injured or taken captive or worse. Don't cry." He took her in his arms again. "We will pray that doesn't happen. We will also pray for a short conflict and a fast resolution. I determine to write as often as possible. I promise your lovely face will not fade from my memory, and as I fall asleep every night I'll think of you. I need you to be brave and I have another request."

She looked up into his eyes. Tears cascaded down her cheeks. "What?"

He cradled her face and wiped her tears with his thumb. "Brutus. I want you to take care of Brutus. My mother doesn't care for the beast and he is in love with you, as I am. He is also a great deterrent. He will defend you to his death. You helped me raise him and train him from a puppy. Brutus will be yours when we are married anyway, so he might as well live here with you now. Also, one less thing for me to worry about while I am gone. You take care of him the best."

"I want to argue with you. I want to knock some sense into your hard head. We should get married right now!"

"My sweet Prudence, please don't argue with me. We have never had a fight. Please don't start one now. I can't fight you. It would break my heart. You mean all the world to me and I don't want our last word to be filled with harshness. We may say something neither of us truly feels and cause hurt. If I didn't feel this was right, I would not have said as much." He sighed. "Now, will you take care of Brutus?"

She nodded.

"Can you give me a smile?"

Her lips quivered into a semblance of a smile. He smoothed them with his finger. "I love your pout. I love your brown eyes. I feel I might drown in the deep pools." He ran a finger across her brow. "I love your smooth, strong, determined forehead."

He captured her in his arms one last time.

He released her. "We should find your missing family and give them my decision."

She stood with him. "Our decision, my love. I would rather run away with you but I trust you and give you my confidence and respect."

Those words took him to the edge, his resolve shaken. He embraced her and claimed her sweet lips. Completely out of breath, her let her go. "You gave me a gift far above anything I could ever hope for. Your trust and faith in me. Thank you. Now, before I change my mind, take me to your parents."

He walked beside her as close as possible without touching. Her parents had taken residence in her father's study. "Father, Mother, we need to tell you something. Oliver, will you please?"

Oliver smiled at her before turning toward her parents. "We decided to postpone the wedding until we can be reunited after this mess with Britain is cleared up. Please know I have your daughter's wellbeing in mind. We desire to be together for a very long time and don't want a separation right after we say our vows."

Her mother's eyebrows had shot up to her hairline. "What? I just gave my permission for a morning wedding, tomorrow!" She rose.

Her husband put his hand on her shoulder. "Dear, I think these two made a sound and mature decision that is theirs to make. I commend them. This world we know is about to change and they will rebuild it their way, together, after the dust settles."

"Thank you, Father. Mother, please understand

our position and stand with us on it."

"Of course. If this is truly what you want, I will stand by you." Beulah moved over and took Prudence into a teary embrace.

Prudence faced the ceiling from the softness of her bed. The fluff of down had become her place to contemplate and have a good cry. Both would be needed. The tears ran freely down into her ears but she barely realized they were there.

She trusted Oliver. She did! Her heart might break knowing they were waiting an innumerable amount of time. A year? Two? More? Unthinkable. Devastating. How would she survive without him near? To look upon? To touch? To feel his fervent love in a kiss?

They had always been close friends. She had loved him since she could remember. Men will be men and try to solve all the world's problems with more than words. Action was what men strived for. She appreciated Oliver's willing spirit to face things head on but right now she wished him different. Safe. Well? Didn't she? No. She wanted him the way he was and had been all his life. Strong, independent, fearless, and a protector of his loved ones and what was right. Handsome with his long brown hair and clean shaven, strong chin. His eyes were dark with flecks of gold. Intense.

She wiggled into a better position. The tears dried, determination filled her as she realized she needed to be brave for his sake, as well as for her family and herself. Brutus. And Brutus, the great huge English Mastiff. She smiled. He would be a good companion and a wonderful watch dog, if the need arose.

The location of the light of the moon, from her bedroom window, told her the night was waning. Sleep, though elusive, needed to be grasped if she would be of any use to anyone in the long hours of the day. Prudence rolled to her side, got comfortable, and closed her eyes from the shadows in the room and the shadows of what was to come.

The maid came in with a tray, waking her for the day. Prudence stretched from the position she had not moved from since receding from thought and opened her eyes.

"Good morning, Fanny. What do you have for me this morning?"

Fanny smiled. "Molly cooked you an egg and buttered you a thick slice of her warm bread. Right from the oven it is. A cup of coffee sweetened by love as we have no sugar. She sends you well wishes and asks if you would care to tap a tree for syrup this fine day?"

Prudence laughed. "Maybe I'll find a leprechaun who will grant me three wishes too."

Fanny caught her eye and giggled. "I'll tell her. She will be missing her Ireland though."

"The sweet maple will not yield its syrup until after the thaws, I'm afraid. Black coffee is wonderful. At least 'tis hot. Thank you for bringing it right up and thank our Molly for her kind but misdirected suggestion."

Prudence ate her mid meal and dressed for a ride on her dear Hautboy. She headed out to the already saddled friend. The horse had a smooth gait and loved the morning runs as well as she did.

Winded and hot but with fingers and cheeks cold and her breath a vapor, she rounded the bend to head for home. Across the fields she glimpsed the hat of a rider. She spurred Hautboy forward to intercept. As she drew near she recognized the rider and horse. Oliver and Whistlejacket.

She reined in and waited. Bending low, she whispered to Hautboy, "Good boy. Oliver and your friend are here." The horse flicked its ears.

Whistlejacket came to a stop a mere foot away. "Prudence, I thought I might catch you out this morning. I received my uniform and head out later this morning. May I come call on my way?"

"Oliver. So soon?"

"I'm afraid so, beloved. Too soon we must part. Pray it will be a brief parting. Now, I must race home and tell my family and pack a few necessary items. Shall I see you in an hour's time?"

"Yes."

Oliver led his horse closer to Prudence and leaned in. The anticipated kiss held passion mingled with sadness. She willed herself not to cry.

He ended the kiss and took off in a gallop. Prudence watched him until he disappeared in the trees.

Chapter 5

Prudence walked down the long staircase toward the sound of her beloved Oliver's voice.

Earlier, she had galloped home to freshen up and put on a clean gown with a pearl stomacher. She wanted his last glimpse of her to be dressed in her finest.

Each step took Prudence closer to saying her good-byes and she was excited but saddened by the prospect. Excited to see him. Saddened that this would be the last time. For how long? She didn't know.

Oliver came into her view as he spoke to her father and mother. He stood tall and handsome in his uniform consisting of a long brown coat, white waistcoat, shirt, and breeches. His muscular legs were covered in white stockings down to brown boots. His broad shoulders, stretching the material, appeared to be able to carry the weight of the world.

His hands held his brown cocked hat at the small of his back. A dagger and saber were attached at his belt. Prudence drank in the sight before her as if this last glimpse of him, before he left, would parch her soul for a lifetime.

At the bottom of her descent, he looked up and their eyes met. She couldn't breathe. Time stood still. Had she been able to move, she would have flown into his arms, not caring for propriety. He broke the spell and came to her. His hand reached out for hers. She placed her lace covered ones into his strong warm fingers.

Again, her parents left the couple alone in the entry hall. She vaguely realized her aunt and grandmother were also missing this parting. His head came down to kiss her gloved hand. "Just a minute." She said as she withdrew her hand, pulled the glove off, and handed him her cool fingers. "Much better."

Oliver grinned and searched her eyes. Then lifted her hand to kiss not the back but her palm and up her wrist as far as the sleeve at her elbow would allow. A tremor sailed up her spine.

Oliver raised his head. "I wish things were different and we were man and wife. It pains me that the world has decided to tilt into this objective, although I agree we need to stand up to this tyranny. But I will miss my beauty before me." He placed his hat on the newel post and cradled her cheek in his free hand, rubbing his thumb against her skin. "I have memorized the color of your hair, every curve of your face, the feel of your satin skin, and the taste of your lips. You are my soul mate and I will hurry home as fast as I possibly can." He captured her lips in a kiss of a promise for a future where they would be together.

He turned and grasped his hat as he strode out the door before she had a chance to say a word.

She slipped down to sit on the bottom step and erupted in quiet sobs that shook her body.

An arm went around her shoulders and she looked up to her father's strong face. "My girl." He placed her head on his shoulder. "Cry all you want. He will be back. Oliver is wise and strong and the Lord will go with him."

A bark followed by a whine reached her ears. "Brutus!" Prudence jumped up and ran to let the beast in. She stooped and he swiped his tongue over the tears on her chin. His tail hung low. A whine came from deep in his throat. "You know he's gone. You and I will mourn until he returns. Thank you for coming."

"We brought over his bowl and the structure they made for him, but I suspect you will spoil him and he will remain indoors with you." Her father smiled.

Prudence nodded. "Thank you, Father. Will Mother object?"

"It is all right with me and I told Emeline and my mother that this is the way it should be," her mother said.

Prudence hugged her. "Thank you, Mama."

"You haven't called me that for years. I like it."

Prudence smiled and leaned her cheek against her mother's. "I think I'm old enough now, I don't need to prove it anymore. You always were Ma or

Mama in my heart even when my lips spoke the formal Mother."

The three hugged again. "Supper is ready when you are, sweet Prudence. Come. Try to eat," her father said.

They went into the dining room and found Aunt Emeline and Granny waiting.

After the meal, her family retired for the night. They said their good nights with a special hug and message from her father, "You are strong, my child, and the Lord is watching over you both. In a few years this will all have seemed a vapor in time."

Restless, Prudence went out into the cool night. The stars, scattered across the sky like small diamonds, twinkled a brilliance that at some other time would make her happy. "Lord, you see this sky from your angle above. Does the sky appear the same or is it vastly different? My sweet Oliver is under these stars somewhere. You are aware of everything he does and place he goes. Please watch over him. Keep him warm, fed, and safe. Those things are a need. I need him to come home to me. I miss him so deeply and he has only been gone a few hours which seems a year. Is that how this will be? My loneliness stretching out the time to infinity while he is gone? Oh Lord, help me keep everything in perspective. Keep me strong.

"Father announced he, too, is leaving in a fortnight. I need to be strong to hold this family together. Give me strength in body, mind, and emotions. Only you know what the future holds."

A twig snapped in the trees a few yards from where she stood. She stiffened and peered into the darkness. Brutus shot past her into the brush with a low growl.

Chapter 6

Brutus trotted back from the shadows and clamped his teeth on Prudence's skirt, tugging her to the shadowed tree line. She took a guarded step and out came a figure of a man. She pulled up and placed her hand on the dog's head and whispered, "Brutus, who is it?"

Brutus let go of her skirt. A whine and a tail thump was his reply.

The form got closer. "Prudence, it's me, Jonas."

A wave of relief swept from her warm forehead to her toes. Oliver's brother. Why? And why not from the front of the house? In the dark? These questions swirled around faster than a dust devil on a July day.

"Jonas, is everything all right? Is your mother well?"

"Mother is well. I decided on a walk on this

fine evening and ended up next to your property, and that's when Brutus found me."

"Really? Forty-eight acres separates us at that point."

He laughed. "Are you going to invite me in?"

"Come."

She turned. Brutus walked beside her to the back door of the house, and into the kitchen. They entered a warm room with fireplace blazing and scattered candles aglow creating wisps of smoke. Molly, busy righting the kitchen, stopped and asked, "Would you like some coffee? I have a few morsels I can serve."

"Coffee would be lovely, Molly. Thank you. I'm sure Jonas has had his evening meal."

Prudence pulled out a chair and sat, indicating the one across the table for Jonas. He took the seat offered. "Black."

"How are your parents?"

"Fine. Father will leave for his regimental training in a day or so."

"Are you going?" The coffee cup she received warmed and comforted her hands. "Thank you, Molly."

"My mind's not made up. Someone should tend to matters here and I'm not as riled as they. I believe I'll weigh my options on how things proceed."

"I suppose."

"This kitchen is cozy." He swiveled his eyes from the fire to her face. "I love the way the firelight plays across your hair and features. My brother is a lucky man."

Prudence fiddled with her cup.

"Prude, if you need anything while your father and Oliver are away, I'll be right here. Yes, I think that is the best place to be." His eyes trailed from her lips down her throat and past, making her draw her shawl closer.

Prudence hated it when people shortened her name and the smug expression and his traveling eyes made her want to toss her hot coffee at him. "You would be better served next to your father and brother who know where their loyalties lie." She took a large gulp of the hot liquid and firmly set her cup down. "Well, it is late and I have an early morning." She stood. "Shall I give you a lantern to light your steps back home?"

"I'll be fine in the dark. Is Brutus staying here? He appears comfortable in front of your fire."

She looked over at Brutus who was down on his haunches, head on his front paws, and eyes alert. "Good boy, Brutus. Please see Jonas out."

The dog leapt up and trotted to the door. Prudence opened it and stood to the side. Jonas rose and walked to the opening. "Thank you for the coffee and conversation. I hope to enjoy your company again soon."

"Don't trouble yourself. We will be fine. You have your own lands to attend to. Good night."

Prudence closed and bolted the door. Brutus waited for the next command. "Come, dear boy. Bed. Sleep well, Molly. Thank you for staying." She carried the cups to the wash basin. "Would you like for me to wash these for you?"

"Nil. I'll take care in the morn."

Prudence nodded and headed toward her room with the dog on her heals.

A time of reflection on her soft bed brought her to ask why Jonas gave her the unsettling feeling. The rumors around town or the stories of his antics and escapades shared by Oliver? A roaming lad had grown into a man whose reputation led men to keep their daughters away. Surely, as she was promised to his brother and a ring graced her finger, he would leave her alone. The veiled promise of unwanted attention made her skin crawl.

"Lord, please keep him away and busy on his own land or better yet, send him off to march with the other fellows. Give my Oliver a restful night and safety in the day."

"Prudence, will you give me the honor of becoming my wife?"

Those words reverberated around Prudence's head, keeping her going over the time Oliver had been gone. She missed him terribly.

An age ago, it seemed, they had strolled in the garden of her stately home on the plantation near the Monocacy River in close proximity to Frederick. She wished for word from him.

Brutus kept her company. He loved to play. When he got the hankering, he took hold of her skirt and tugged her toward the door. His teeth firmly clamped but he was gentle not to tear the fabric. Laughter escaped her lips most times and she relented. On some occasions a rebuke made him drop her skirt. "Not now, Brutus." Eager to please, he released and sat wagging his tail. A great companion with his undying love and fun antics. Oliver had raised him and, for no other reason, made her love the animal but he had become one of the family. His nearness was a comfort on the lonely days of pining for her Love.

Three letters came a few weeks after her father left. One from her father to her mother and two addressed to her from Oliver. She rushed to the privacy of her bedroom and flounced onto the bed, crawling to the foot to where the light from the window reached the best.

March 6, 1776

My dearest Prudence,

I trust you are well. I am surrounded by men eager to get into the fray, whenever and wherever that is. We drill and march. My bayonet has been thrust through sacks of hay over and over. I remember the time your auntie got tangled in one and a smile replaces the determined look, I suppose.

I miss you, my darling. I long to see you and hold you. I think of you every day and your face is the last my mind pictures before sleep takes hold. We head out at dawn tomorrow. Always closer to where the British are and where we will eventually be needed if indeed a war breaks out.

All my love,

O.D.

Prudence refolded the letter and opened the second.

March 26, 1776

My sweet one, I long to touch you. You are in my thoughts every waking moment. I hope you are getting my letters. Finding an honest courier to risk his life carrying this to you is difficult indeed. Anyone possessing correspondence and intercepted can be hung for treason. I did not expect this. I write at least three times a week but can only send a few. I keep them to give you later. Just writing my thoughts helps me feel you are near reading over my shoulder or listening to my heart.

I love you with my whole being!

I pray for you to have strength and courage through this separation. Providence is in control and will get us through. Have faith.

Love,

O.D.

Prudence wiped tears from her eyes and folded the page and placed it in a wooden box her father made. He had given it to her years ago after sanding and oiling it to a satin finish. She lovingly ran her fingers across the surface. "Father. I miss you too." She slipped off the bed and headed to check on her mother and to hear the news from her father.

"Your father is fine and attending to the men's needs as a parson can do. He sends his love." Her mother blushed. *There must be more in the letter that she doesn't want to share.* Prudence smiled to herself realizing both women missed their men and intimate thoughts were shared between the couples and were not for others' eyes.

Months passed since her father took his leave. Many times, Prudence cried along with the three women. Her father had left her mother in charge of the foreman Boon, who would run the place while he was gone. Boon had been with the Ainsworths since his birth and his father and mother had a cottage on the Ainsworth property. Robert, his father, worked as the blacksmith while Lucy, his mother, oversaw the household staff. Molly and Lucy had a silent agreement. Molly was her own boss. Most times, Molly held top rung.

Prudence smiled, thinking of the jibing they did, knowing full well they liked and respected each other. Human nature was a curious thing.

Boon worked his way up through the ranks because of his hard work and honesty. As a bachelor, he preferred to sleep with the other men in the long house. At times her father relied on him as his own son.

They were a blessing while her father had been gone. The plantation operated as smoothly as a well-greased axle on a wagon.

War was declared in April and the dreaded beast had captured more than lives. Food and supplies ran low. Thank the Lord they were mostly self-sufficient.

A trip to Gibson's store brought more than cash for the eggs. A letter! As soon as she climbed onto the carriage, she opened the letter.

August 23, 1776

My sweet Prudence,

I pray this letter reaches you and finds you well. We traveled miles through forests, glens, and across rivers to reach Colonel Smallwood and the other seven companies. We are now considered the Maryland Battalion and assigned to the Continental

Army.

So far we have drilled until we drill in our sleep. I believe my musket is permanently attached to my hand. I am one of the lucky ones because of Whistlejacket, who is most coveted even by the Captains. He is a mighty animal. The grass has been sufficient as of now for his large appetite. I'm thankful for the winter to be gone for that purpose. I do not know how I'll provide for him next winter if this war lasts that long. We head out tomorrow, soon to be reassigned.

The men I serve with are strong and unified. We have a common goal and deep faith that God will get us through this war. Or rations are adequate and weapons in top notch conditions. I sleep under a wool blanket and gaze at the stars, thinking of you.

I miss my betrothed. Thoughts of you, beautiful Prudence, fill my mind. My fingers itch to run across your cheek and through your brown tresses. I yearn for a taste of your sweet lips again and to linger there in a never ending kiss.

Eternally yours,
O.D.

She refolded the letter and slipped it into her satchel which also held a few supplies and coin from the eggs. Prudence cradled the large head of her furry companion. "Brutus, a letter from your master. He is well. I know you miss him." She gathered up the reins and clicked her tongue. The carriage rolled forward.

August. So long ago. The celebration of Christmas is near. Where was he now? She told herself to be thankful she had received news. So many men gone and women waiting to hear. Mists of fear swirled in her mind and heart. Her courage and trust waned.

At home she handed her mother the other letter. A short one from her father. Seems he is tending to wounds as well as souls, being trained in both. Father had not met up with either Oliver or Oliver's father, Hezekiah.

Rebecca Duke had occasionally stopped by or Prudence and her family went to her home to check on her. Jonas had been absent the times she arrived at the Duke plantation. A great relief.

Their plantation was a bit larger and they had more workers to run it smoothly. Unfortunately at both plantations, men had been drifting away since April. For the first time, Prudence worried what would happen if they lost all the menfolk.

A knock on her door brought her out of her musings. She again folded the letter she had reread and placed it along with the others in her special wooden box. "Yes?"

Fanny entered. "Miss Prudence, Silas sent me to inform you of a caller."

"Who?"

"Mr. Cox. He asked for you."

"Where is Mother?"

"She is out with Boon."

"Grandmother?"

"In the parlor. She said to tell you she will be by your side and has a pistol under her apron."

"Good old Granny. And Auntie?"

"Waiting in the dining room, just in case, holding a pistol."

Prudence laughed as she led the way from her room and down the stairs with Brutus at her heels.

Chapter 7

Prudence straightened her shoulders and sobered her features before entering the parlor. Sure enough, Granny sat with her hand resting on an obvious bulge under her apron. Prudence resisted the urge to grin.

"Why, Mr. Cox, what brings you out on this fine day?"

He turned from the fireplace and faced her. "An offer I'm sure you will not refuse."

"I don't understand. We don't want to purchase any cattle or land at this time."

He sniggered. "You wouldn't have the means. I aim to put some cash in your pocket."

"I'm sure *we* have nothing you could compensate us for."

"Land."

Prudence stiffened and raised an eyebrow. Brutus looked at her then back to the man. She placed her head on his broad head.

"The land your cattle graze. Sell your cattle and I'll take the strip off your hands. You benefit with cash and less workers are needed. As I see it, your men abandoned you and this would profit us both." He leaned his arm on the fireplace mantel, appearing to relax, but she had seen him eye the dog.

"First of all, Mr. Cox, Mother is the one you should be speaking to and I can tell you she won't sell our land. The cattle are in good hands and we are as well."

"This is where you come in, young lady. Your mother will need encouragement to appreciate the broad picture."

Prudence tilted her head.

"I've been privy to speech about *harm* possibly to come to you dear sweet ladies because of where your men folk place their allegiance. You, because of the Dukes, and your mother and the rest because of the simpleton leaning of your father."

"Granny. Hold that thing still, I wouldn't want it to go off accidentally." Prudence didn't take her eyes off the man before her.

He swiveled his head in her granny's direction, straightened, and held up his hand. "Stay calm. Put it away before someone gets hurt."

Granny wiggled the pistol. "I guess you better be on your way if you don't want to experience an accident."

A low growl came from Brutus.

Cox glanced at him and back at Prudence.

"You women need to heed my offer before the

land will come by me some other way." He gave them both a curled sneer.

"Now would be a good time to leave." Prudence moved out of the way, keeping her hand on Brutus and tilted her head toward the door. Silas appeared, holding the man's hat. "Thank you Silas. Please escort our neighbor off our property."

A musket swing up in Silas's other hand. "Yes, mistress."

"Humph. I'll go but you think about my offer. It may not be as sweet next time around."

Boon poked his head into the room. "Mr. Cox, I believe your horse is in need of fetching. It appears he slipped from the tether."

The man all but ran from the room, snatching his hat from Silas on the way.

Prudence followed the men with Granny right behind. Cox skimmed down the front steps and hastened after his horse, who seemed to be off on an adventure, trotting out the yard.

At that moment her mother entered from the back. "What's all the commotion?"

Prudence and Granny laughed. The men grinned. "We had a visit from Mr. Cox. His greedy little mind thinks we need to sell him our grazing land. After, of course, we sell our cattle. He gave a not-so-veiled threat, I'm afraid."

"What kind?"

"I assume his loyalty to the crown and ours to our liberty places us at odds and he thinks we and our property are his ravin. He implied others were not keen on our allegiance."

"Why did he come to you?"

"He assumed I needed to talk you into this absurd proposition. What are your thoughts?"

"He is delusional if he thinks I would part with any of Samuel's holdings. This property, as you are very aware, has been in his family's possession since the crossing of the Atlantic to get away from tyranny. This is something loyalists don't understand. We remember because of the lessons our grandfathers learned and taught us."

"Of course." Prudence paused. "One thing we should glean and heed from his visit. Well, two. One is we need to be vigilant in protecting life and limb as well as our holdings."

"And the second?" her mother asked.

"He is determined to get what he wants and will most likely stoop to whatever means necessary."

Prudence's mother nodded. "I follow. Mother, you agree with Prudence's assessment?"

"Yes. He is extremely sure of himself, until I held up my pistol of course." Granny waved the steel weapon.

"Good for you, Mother. We should all be armed. Boon? Silas? Agreed?"

The men held up their weapons. Boon said, "I'll tell my parents and the rest."

"Boon, thank you for loosening Cox's horse. Watching him scurry away was a reward. Good to have you on our side," Prudence said.

He grinned, tapped his forehead in a salute, turned, and left the way he had come, through the front door. Boon skimmed the tree line and up and down the drive with his gaze. He nodded. At what?

Prudence had no idea. He headed around to the back and out of sight.

Silas left to do whatever needed doing.

Beulah said, "Let's find Emeline and get a strategy together. This is our house, after all, and our responsibility."

"I'm here." Emeline came through the door. "I heard the whole thing and followed Cox out of the yard. He didn't see me." She laughed. "Too sure of himself. And uneducated as to who we are. I'll take the first watch if that's all right with you, Beulah."

Prudence's mother hugged her sister. "Dear Emeline, thank you for being my sister and a sneaky, untrusting woman."

The others laughed as Emeline frowned. "I'm not sure you gave me a compliment but I'll take it as such."

Chapter 8

Quiet months passed on the Ainsworth plantation. The monotony stirred a restlessness in Prudence, so she mounted Hautboy to check on fencing. It was something she desired to do and assured Boon she would let him know if anything needed his attention. This gave her a purpose to ride.

As long as she could remember, she worked alongside her father. Every aspect of the plantation she had learned at his side. All four ladies had been taught not only to defend themselves, but if a need arose, they were also armed with the ability to do any and all of the chores associated with the property. Father taught Prudence how to ride, tend fences, scatter seed, and explained all the rudiments of how the plantation worked. Some of her favorite times had been those riding out with her father to check the animals and crops and the fences.

The cows munched on hay as she checked their

boundary. The fence appeared in well repair. She tried to shake it in places, to no avail. Sturdy. Her father had made sure himself before leaving but with the fall winds she needed peace of mind. No sense inciting their neighbor to bring again his "offer."

Heading back to the house, she rode on the side of the fields opposite to the border of her property and the Duke plantation. The fields laid bare waiting for sowing. Next week they would plant and pray for a good harvest. Seed had been purchased with funds her father set aside for that purpose.

Her eyes trailed to a large maple where she had met Oliver on several occasions. Oh, how she missed him! The longing in her heart and mind sometimes was unbearable. A tear slid unbidden down her cheek. A figure emerged from behind the tree. *Can it be?* Prudence shook her head. "Jonas."

Brutus had his nose in the air. "Do you smell him, boy? Should we turn or would that be rude?"

"Prudence!"

"Too late. He's coming."

Brutus stayed beside her. She decided to keep her mount.

"You look lovely today, dear Prudence."

"Thank you. How is your mother?"

"She's well. I'd rather talk about you."

"I received a letter from your brother. Did you receive word from him?"

He shook his head. "Not even a scrap."

"Your father?"

"Yes. He is doing well and met up with Oliver

somewhere in Pennsylvania."

"Will you join a battalion?"

"Not at this time. The fields need my attention and I would hate to leave Mother alone."

Prudence scanned the brown earth. "When are you going to plant?"

"Soon. You?"

"Next week."

"I'll see you then? I assume you will be helping?"

"We all pitch in where needed. I should head back." She turned her horse and said over her shoulder, "Please give your mother my regards. I hope to call on her soon."

He snatched the bridle of her horse. "My brother is a very lucky man. You're beautiful. Handsome on a horse. That habit suites you." He scanned her outfit lingering where he should not.

She pulled back on the reins. Hautboy whinnied. Brutus barked. Prudence said, "Easy boy. Jonas, let go."

"I shall see you next week, if not before." He dropped the reins and jerked his horse around to gallop away.

"Brutus, why does he bother me so?" The dog's hackles were raised. "He concerns you also. Good boy." She reached over the side and patted the furry head. A calm came over her. "You would protect me even from Oliver's brother. I think you deserve a treat. Come, I'll race you to the house for a big bowl of leftover stew!"

She leaned into the saddle and gave Hautboy his head. The horse and dog matched strides to the stable. Prudence slipped off Hautboy. "Thank you, Kitch. Please give Hautboy a good brushing and some oats."

"Aye." The groom snagged the bridle, and murmured sweet nothings to the horse as he led Prudence's mount to the waiting stall.

In the kitchen, Brutus devoured a bowl of leftovers before Prudence sat down to her refreshment of apple slices and strong coffee. Her mother, aunt, and granny joined her. She told them about the fences. "I ran into Jonas and he has heard from his father, who is well, but not Oliver. I haven't received a letter for quite a while. I miss him and am anxious for a word from him."

"I may as well tell you," her mother began, paused, and slid a folded paper across the table toward her. "I got this while you were out."

"Who is it from?"

"Your father."

"Why are you handing it to me?"

"He speaks of Oliver on that page. It's addressed to you."

Pierced with dread, Prudence slowly opened the page and began reading.

My dear daughter,

I saw Oliver yesterday for a brief moment. He appears in good health and spirt. And sends his love. He spoke highly of the men he serves as well as the men who train next to him. There seems to have been an incident in which he has need of a new horse. In the rain the men were moving the troops and canons up an embankment. The rope pulling a canon snapped and the heavy monster slid in the mud and fell against Whistlejacket, throwing Oliver. Whistlejacket's leg got broken in the accident. Oliver only sustained scrapes from the bush he landed on. Oliver had to shoot his beloved horse. This was a difficult thing for Oliver to do but necessary, I'm afraid. He is trying to find a new mount but it may take time as they are in a short and coveted supply.

Oliver said he wrote and told you but he suspected the man he gave the letter to deliver simply kept the money and burned it. Men are more righteous and keep their word to me, "A Man of God," as they call me here. I wanted you to know of this trial of Oliver's and to pray the good Lord sends a horse.

Your loving father

"Oh, Mama!" Prudence crossed her arms on the table and slumped over, burying her head, as sobs racked her body, releasing all the pent-up emotions from the months gone by.

Chapter 9

Prudence lifted her tear-streaked face toward her mother, who had taken her into her arms. "Oh my sweet Oliver, how sad you must be! Mother, how can we help? He needs to be equipped with a horse."

"If he were home he could choose from a number of studs," her mother said.

"That's it! One of his horses!"

"Prudence, you can't be thinking of taking one to him. Dangerous and out of the question! Your father and Oliver would forbid it!"

"You're right, it will be dangerous, but someone else should and shall go, if I, with the help of his mother, can convince him."

Her mother frowned. "Who?"

Granny chimed in. "You're thinking Jonas."

"Yes. It's his duty and since he has not united

with the cause, he needs to grab this chance to help his fellow man, especially, because Oliver is his own flesh and blood!" Excitement pulsated through Prudence.

"My dear, that will be an accomplishment to enlist Jonas's help. I hope you are up to the challenge."

Prudence stood. "I am! I will head over to call on his mother, post-haste!"

Granny stood. "I perceive you need an ally to convince those two."

"Mother, you are the most persuasive of us, you go with our diplomatic Prudence." Beulah quirked her lip.

"Mother dear, I will be as diplomatic as I possibly can, and then bribe, cajole, and if I have to, pressurize them into the right decision." Prudence stormed to the door. "Granny, are you ready? Mama and Auntie, pray I calm a bit before I storm the castle!"

Granny guffawed. "A bit more spice is what you might need."

"Mother, you are supposed to be helping, not enticing. We will pray for you both!" Prudence's mother said.

Prudence graced them with a huge grin, swung out the door, and marched to the barn for their horses.

Over the fields, Prudence prayed for the right words and attitude to convey the necessity for Jonas to help his brother. She glanced at Granny and detected the same spirit in her. *And thank you Lord for this strong, godly woman. I am blessed.*

Prudence dismounted Hautboy and wrapped his reins over the rail as her granny did the same with Sweetdawn.

She strode to the door and knocked. The Duke's butler, Daniel, opened the door. "Why, Miss Prudence, we didn't expect you today. I'll let Ma'am know you are here. I see you brought Mrs. Bartlett. Please wait in the parlor and I'll retrieve refreshments." He led them to the room adjacent to the entry. "Please have a seat, it may be a few minutes."

Prudence leaned into her granny and whispered, "Shall we ask for Jonas too?"

Daniel turned to go as Granny spoke out the side of her mouth. "Not yet. Let's try to make this her idea."

"I suspect that's the best move. I'm glad we are on the same team," she whispered back and kissed her granny's cheek.

They sat on the settee and waited. About fifteen minutes later a tray was brought in to them and a few minutes more, in swooped Oliver's mother dressed as if she were attending a ball. Prudence felt a little uncomfortable knowing she wore her riding habit from earlier. She had not stopped to change nor bothered to take the carriage around on the roads as that would have added another half hour to the drive. She glanced at Granny who sat tall and regal in her work dress. She wanted to laugh or cry at the scene. Instead, she took the cue and sat forward, stiffening her spine as any princess would.

Her grandmother said, "Thank you for receiving us, Rebecca, on this late afternoon. I hope we didn't interrupt anything important. Were you about to call on someone?"

"Oh…" She smoothed out her skirt. "You caught me going through my clothes and I decided to keep this one on. How are you, Prudence?" She nodded to each lady. "Keziah?"

"We came with word from my son-in-law who mentioned your son and we thought you might be interested," Granny said.

Prudence added, "Yes, especially as Jonas told me today you have not received a letter from Oliver either."

Eyes wide, Mrs. Duke said, "Please go ahead. I hope it is not despairing."

"Father said Oliver is well and appeared healthy."

She visibly relaxed. "Wonderful. This dreadful time has us all in knots not knowing what may happen to our men. I'm sure you were relieved."

"I am most pleased he is well. There is more. An unfortunate accident happened in which Whistlejacket got injured," said Prudence.

"Gracious! Is it bad? Was Oliver hurt?"

"Oliver was thrown but only received scratches and I'm sure bruises. But I'm afraid Whistlejacket broke his leg and Oliver…"

"Oh no!"

"Yes. He had to put him down."

"My poor boy and Whistlejacket! He used to be one of our finest. You know Oliver broke him and trained him. Such a sad affair. You do get close to your horse especially in times of peril."

Prudence looked at her hands clasped in her lap

and shook her head.

Mrs. Duke asked, "Whatever shall he do?"

"He needs a horse. One that is fearless, tireless, and capable. I know of no stock equal to one like Whistlejacket to measure up as a mount and friend." Prudence sighed.

Granny echoed the sigh for effect. "Yes. A magnificently bred animal. No other could possibly take his place. The breeding and care. You cannot find any worthy. Such a rare thing." She shook her head.

Prudence maintained a straight face at Granny's antics and deepened her sad countenance.

"True. True," said Mrs. Duke.

Prudence asked, "Do you have an idea to help your son?"

Mrs. Duke tapped her pursed lips.

Prudence waited, holding her breath. She and Granny didn't move a muscle.

"Our horses are supreme. A difficult thing to replace."

"Yours are the best anywhere," Prudence agreed. "A man is proud and strong on one of your mounts. They are hands taller and muscled where others shrink in their presence. Horses from the Duke stables are worth their weight in gold."

"Precisely. Too bad… wait! Why can't he have one of his own horses?"

"What a wonderful idea! You would save your son's life indeed! But how?"

"Well, we can't go." She pointed to herself and Prudence.

Prudence tilted her head down and shook it.

"Jonas!"

Prudence almost jumped out of her skin at Mrs. Duke's exclamation. Right then, he walked in. "Did I hear my name?"

His mother hopped up and clasped his hands. "Yes. You must go. There is no time. He needs you. What one? I know, Dashwood. Oliver broke him as well. Jonas, hurry. You must pack!"

"Mother, what's wrong? Come sit back down and tell me all about it." He helped her to sit and keeping her hand and sat next to her. He glanced with a frown at Prudence.

"Jonas, your brother needs you. You are the only one to manage this. It's your duty. Your father would be proud. I would be proud."

"Why, pray tell, would my brother in the army need me?"

"Why, for a horse, of course."

"What your sweet mother is referring to is, Whistlejacket broke his leg and Oliver had to shoot him. Oliver is in need of a horse and your horses are not rivaled by any other. Your mother thinks it's a fantastic idea to send you with one. That way, you can take a closer look at the *cause* and ascertain how your brother fairs and give him a mount superior to any he might find. You might save his life. You would be a hero."

"Fantastic, yes. Crazy, definitely. Are you three serious? This is ludicrous. Dangerous. And well…" He smiled. "Sure. If I get something out of it."

Prudence felt his eyes devouring her. Her face grew hot. Indignant, she wanted to storm out, but Oliver's life depended on this moment.

Keziah stood and stepped in front of her, facing the Dukes. "I never realized how amenable you might be to the task at hand. Your brother, I'm sure, will thank you and you can work that out between the two of you at a later date. You can't speak to him at present but I'm sure between your father and your brother something will be worked out, don't you agree, Rebecca?"

Rebecca Duke said, "Of course. This is family, after all, Jonas. Time is short. There is much to do. We need to put together provisions." She stood. "That's settled. Thanks for coming, ladies, and bringing news of my son's necessity. Jonas will leave first light."

Prudence stood and kept on the side of Granny, away from Jonas. They made their way to their horses. As she placed her foot into the stirrup, a hand braced her elbow and another clasped around her waist, lifting her. Soon she was up on the horse. Jonas didn't release her waist. In a low voice he said, "I will want compensation. Be ready."

She backed Hautboy and trotted out of the yard as tears stung her eyes.

Chapter 10

Oliver carried his ink and quill to a rock beside the stream near where the men had camped. He sat on the rock and scanned the distance though his thoughts were hundreds of miles away.

Oliver dipped his quill and began a letter. He wanted to state everything clearly yet knew he should shade things for her protection.

My dearest Prudence,

Nearby stands Dashwood munching grass. He's an intelligent and strong beast and I need to thank you for his delivery. Jonas is here speaking to our commanding officer about his travels.

Jonas said he will get compensated for his trek across the miles. I'm not sure what he is alluding to. His mind works on a different plane than that of myself. To think we came from the same loins is indeed remarkable. Jonas should stay with us because every available weapon is in need but I'm afraid he will navigate back home. He said he is needed to keep the home fires burning. Of course, mother is capable and she has help with our trustworthy Daniel, who gave me his word he would not abandon her no matter what.

I saw Father a while back and he is well. I wish we had orders to fight together but alas we have different skills and they need him elsewhere. He is an honest and solid man whom I look up to. Unfortunately, I only came in contact with your father one brief time, right after the accident which took Whistlejacket from me. Your father was a great comfort to me. Such a sad state of affairs. He is probably why you were privy to my quest to find a new horse. I feel you are not receiving my letters.

On this sunny day, I sit out by a beautiful stream and dream of a walk here with you hand in hand but alas, I can only write my thoughts. You are always on my mind and heart. I think over the many conversations we've had through the years and remember every movement of your body and expression of your face. I dream of having those spirited conversations with the woman I love who is full of wisdom and grace. I long to hear your sweet voice. Touch your soft silky hair and skin. View the sparkle in your eyes and taste the dew of your rosy lips. My arms long to hold you close to me, never to let you go again. This war has only begun and I wish to God it were over.

I will not be at liberty to write for a long while. Last August, after I sent my last letter to you, we had a difficult order to bombard the British while Washington and his troops escaped Long Island.

Because I was one of a few who made it out, I've been under scrutiny and given a special assignment. I leave at dawn. Jonas came at the exact time I needed a reliable horse. Providence granted my fervent prayer. You were part of that prayer and you worked skillfully with my mother and brother to send Dashwood. I'm sure by the time you were through, mother thought it her idea. Jonas thinks so.

I pray as I close this that you will indeed receive this from my brother's hand. He is my representative to your family and mine.

I love you to the ends of the world,
O.D.

Oliver folded the paper and sealed it in wax before finding Jonas. "Please see that my Prudence gets this." He handed his brother the letter. "I have orders to head elsewhere. Please be careful. Arrive safely home to Mother and give both her and Prudence my love." He took his brother in an embrace.

"I intend to personally give this to Prudence, never fear. Where are you headed?"

"I'm afraid I'm not at liberty to say. Are you sure you won't stay? We could use your marksmanship and other abilities."

Jonas shook his head. "Brother, this is not my fight. I wouldn't put my heart into it and I'd get myself killed."

"True. A man fights best when he is hell-bent on the outcome. Go in peace and thank you."

The evening waned and Oliver crawled into his bedroll to stare at the stars, needing sleep but unable to succumb. The crickets, frogs, and an occasional fish splashed in the steam. The chorus finally lulled him to sleep.

At dawn, he rode out with a final glance at the sleeping form of his brother. A premonition of trouble brewing raised the hairs on the back of his neck. For whom, he didn't know. Jonas? Prudence? Himself?

The rest of the battalion was up, striking camp, for a long trek toward the enemy's lines. He, on the other hand, headed in another direction. A prayer graced his lips. "Almighty, I need your wisdom and protection as I go into an unknown world on an extremely dangerous mission. Only You know the outcome. I pray I can survive and find my way back to my beloved Prudence. Please keep her safe and help her feel Your presence in her life and trust You. Draw Jonas to Yourself and keep him safe as he travels home. Whatever crisis awaits, we are all in Your hands. Amen."

Months went by. Prudence and Mrs. Duke did not receive word from Oliver or Jonas. The silence almost unnerved Prudence. Had Jonas delivered the horse? Had he joined the ranks and forgotten his pledge to her and his mother? Were the horses stolen and he left to fend for survival? So many questions sailed around her head like a falcon after a sparrow. Life progressed. The crops were being harvested.

One letter had come from her father which spoke of his safety and love for his family. Brutus had grown used to life on the plantation and cavorted around, sometimes arriving home with a bird or other prey in his mouth as a token of love. "Good dog. I'll fix this for your supper." She dressed the bird and cooked it on the spit. After the fowl cooled, she placed it in his dish. Brutus devoured the meat almost in one gulp. She wondered if he needed more food than she gave him.

Prudence stared at the man in front of her. How could he suggest such a thing? The audacity! Jonas had delivered Dashwood to Oliver and now held a wax-sealed letter in his hands, expecting payment.

"No one need know."

"I'll know. So will the Almighty. I won't do what you are suggesting to myself nor Oliver! I'll remain faithful to Oliver the remainder of my days. Your brother no doubt made you swear to deliver this to me." Prudence stiffened her spine and stretched out her arm. "Hand it over."

"Of course, after a bit of fun."

A commotion behind him caused him to turn. Granny stood, legs planted, and pistol pointed at his head. "I would do as she asks or we will retrieve it from your lifeless body. Your choice."

"My dear Mrs. Bartlett, I assure you this was a jest, a mere test to see if the sweet Prudence would keep her vow of chastity." He frowned and shrugged. "I'm only looking out for Oliver's interest." He swiveled back to Prudence. "Here, my dear future sister-in-law, is your letter." He bowed and swept the paper toward her.

Prudence snatched the letter and took a wide

berth around him to stand beside dear Granny. "Thank you, Granny. You can lower your weapon."

"I'll see this young man off our land first."

Granny tipped her head at Jonas who started toward his horse tethered a few yards away. Granny followed and climbed on her horse while keeping her hand on the trigger. Prudence marveled, not for the first time, at the agility of her grandmother. She figured Granny would release him at the boundary of the property.

The two rode away, single file, toward the Duke Plantation. Prudence walked home to read her letter.

At the house, she found Brutus wagging his tail and a small boy sitting next to him with a skinny arm wrapped around him. "Brutus, who do you have here?"

The boy shied away, hiding his slight form behind the giant animal. The door from the kitchen opened and out walked Auntie. "Gafton, Miss Molly has some raisin cookies and wants your opinion on how they taste."

The boy's eyes grew large. "Really? Me?"

"Yes, you scamp. Hurry in while they are hot."

Prudence frowned and placed her hands on her hips. "Who is that boy and why is Molly using precious raisins to make cookies?"

"An honest boy who had been bribed. Come, let's take a walk and I'll fill you in." She took hold of Prudence's arm and led her away from the house. "I assume you met Granny?"

"Yes. But…"

"Let me tell you."

"All right. I'll be patient but please hurry. I received a letter from Oliver that I'm most anxious to read."

"Apparently, the young waif lost his parents and sister by the British and has been roaming and begging for food ever since. He said they came to his small town to gather up all who were not loyal to the crown. The boy's father tried to protect his family and they shot him and torched his house. Gafton's mother shoved the boy out the window right before the roof collapsed. The flames prevented him from trying to rescue them. A soldier tried to catch him but he ran and hid until the troops left. The devastation and the soldiers frightened the child and he has been on the run since."

"Oh my goodness! The poor lad. I don't understand, why is he here?"

"He said a man paid him to coax Brutus into the cellar and lock him in. He did as he was bid. Then, he thought better of it and came to tell us what he did. He told us the story and asked for forgiveness. The dog has been by his side in a protective stance. Brutus seems to sense the heart of the child."

"Who bribed him?"

"Jonas." They said at the same time.

Auntie nodded. "We discovered you left without Brutus and when Granny heard the tale, she deduced you'd be in trouble. She mumbled something about, 'I knew the scoundrel was up to no good, I just didn't figure how low he'd stoop.'"

"What a tale. Jonas planned on Brutus being out of the way. He understood the dog would help me, protect me."

Auntie gasped. "Are you all right? Did he touch you?"

"I'm fine. Thanks to Granny. What shall we do with our visitor? We can't send him out in this cruel world or into Jonas' clutches."

Auntie shook her head. "Your mother thinks Brutus needs a boy to play with and give him exercise. Shall we hire him for room and board?"

Prudence laughed. "A splendid idea. Is Mother with him now?"

"Yes, she waited in the kitchen. He seems to warm up to her the best."

Prudence and Auntie headed to the house so Prudence could get a proper introduction. Granny rode back in the yard as they neared the door. "Granny! Did you have any more trouble with Jonas?"

Granny dismounted. "He went along peacefully. I doubt that is the end. Where was your firearm, Prudence?"

"I was only going to the boulders to meet Oliver's brother. I didn't think I needed a weapon."

"Well, honey, this proves you do indeed. Also, from now on, no more leaving the yard without Brutus and a weapon. Besides Jonas, we can't afford not to be on guard, especially if what our little friend says is true. We might make it to a Redcoat's list."

"You may indeed," a man's voice said.

Prudence, Auntie, and Granny spun around. Mr. Cox stood with a cocky smile on his face and carrying a musket.

Chapter 11

Prudence said, "Mr. Cox, what are you doing here and to what are you referring?"

"I came to strike a bargain. We know where your sympathies lie. I could protect you. Give me the land and I'll tell them differently."

"Give?"

"Yes. I offered to pay you and you refused. Now, your lives and home for the trade of the land. Oh, and I want more than I first spoke of. I drew up the new boundary."

Out of an inner pocket he took out a sheet of paper and held it up in his grimy hands. Prudence stepped forward. The man reeked. Bad liquor and an unwashed body. She willed herself not to swoon as she snatched the paper. "We will read what you wrote and discuss this among ourselves. You must give us time. This is a huge thing to consider."

"Do more than consider if you know what is

good for you. My friends are well versed in plunder and setting fires." He started to leave and stopped. "Oh, women rarely go unscathed." His grating laugh followed him out the yard. He climbed on his mount and rode out.

Later, after Gafton had been tucked into bed, Prudence opened the unforgotten letter from her beloved. Tears slipped down her cheeks as she read his loved-filled words. "Oh Oliver! How I miss you! What special assignment? Oh, I am fearful for you! I miss you, my beloved! I kiss the wind hoping it reaches you. I pray for you!" She placed her head on the crook of her arm and had a good cry. When the tears stopped she washed her face. Another matter needed her attention.

With a heavy heart, Prudence and her womenfolk discussed the issue and read over the proposal.

"Mother, I don't see any way around this. Other families in the province went under more than scrutiny. Mr. Gibson lost his store and a loyalist is in control and running it. They won't purchase our eggs. Mail is never waiting and I'm afraid they burn ours because of who we are and what we stand for. I'm worried we will need to agree. Father will understand. Giving the land and not losing the house and the other acreage is a small price."

"I'm not ready to make this choice. Is there a way we can counter or stall? I have no way of getting a letter to your father for his consent and advice," her mother said.

"Doesn't Samuel need to sign to make it legal?" Auntie asked.

"The British and their loyalist buddies think they have the crown on their side and will no doubt take whatever they want," Granny said.

"That's it! We need to tell Cox we are taking this matter to the Committee of Safety to help and protect us. If we make it sound like we are asking the Committee to decide if the Crown or their fellows has any right to take land for the sake of a promised protection, he may not do anything rash. Cox will wait, not yet sure he wants to make waves with the new committee, and will give us time to plan. No Revolutionist would allow a loyalist to abscond with a patriot's land. I'll send someone to dispatch our letter, post-haste!" Prudence stood in her excitement.

"My dear girl," her mother said, "You make it sound easy and exciting. We have nothing to lose. Please draft the missive using the verbiage you spoke so eloquently and add drama to the fullest."

Prudence drafted the letter over the next two days. An inquiry in town gave her the description of someone who would be willing to carry her letter. She found him. The unimpressive man said, "Such a tale. I'd run Cox in had I the authority. There aren't enough patriots in this pocket of the world. Many enlisted for the cause. Save your money. I'm going to Annapolis and will take this all the way to the desk of Governor Johnson himself, if I've a mind."

"Thank you, sir."

He climbed upon an old nag and placed the letter in his breast pocket.

"I don't know your name."

"Better for you that way. I already forgot yours.

God be with you."

"And you!"

He clicked his tongue and the horse started forward. Prudence watched him. *With that pace he will get there next year. How do I keep Cox from his threat?*

Prudence waited for word. A letter. Something. She had not received anything from the Committee. Not from Oliver. Jonas kept his distance, which was a relief. Cox had been silent. What would be his next move? Three silent months since she handed the unnamed man her petition.

Oliver seemed on her mind constantly. Questions as to where he fought, what he ate, how well he slept, and did he keep warm, painted pictures and swirled across her mind's eye.

A light snow drifted down from the sky. Prudence sat near the window gazing out but not paying heed to the flakes.

"Prudence, why are you so down in the mouth?" Auntie asked.

Startled, Prudence jerked. "Sorry, Auntie. My mind wanders this world thinking of Oliver. I miss him and imagine the things he may be doing." She smiled at her sweet aunt.

"How long has he been silent?"

Prudence cringed at the word silent. "A year and three months since I received the letter Jonas carried from him. Seems like twenty. I'm sure he has written but can't get the letter to me."

"I hope he hasn't been captured. You know what they do to prisoners."

Her mother said, "Please don't talk like that. Prudence is worried enough. We need to have good, positive thoughts." She came over and gave her girl a hug. Her dress had wet splotches on the shoulders and hem.

"Mother, have you been out?"

"Gafton wanted to play in the snow. I wish I had the child's energy. He and your beast are quite wet, I'm afraid. They are drying by the fire in the kitchen. Molly said lunch is ready."

Prudence followed her mother into the kitchen. She ruffled Gafton's sandy curls and patted her furry companion's head. "Did you two enjoy the cold, wet outdoors?"

Brutus answered with his tongue on her hand, and Gafton said, "Yes. He tried to eat the snowballs I threw."

Prudence laughed. "Come get some lunch. I'm sure Molly made your favorite."

She poured soup in Brutus' dish. "Here, boy. The soup is warmer than the snow and better for you."

Prudence sat at the table and accepted her lunch from Molly. She gazed at the lad across from her.

In the months since Gafton appeared on their door step, he had wiggled into their affections. Prudence's mother and Auntie doted on the fellow. They were doing their best to fatten him up which seemed an impossible task especially with the economy in these times of peril. Prudence marveled at the way God had orchestrated the child's life to come to their town and the circumstances which brought him to live in their home. Even Jonas, in his schemes, played a part. Providence redirected and made good out of bad.

If only the Lord would change the course of events in her life so a word from her beloved Oliver would arrive. The ache in her heart felt like an oozing sore no amount of salve could heal.

Memories of his voice, face, and touch echoed in her brain. A yearning to feel his arms around her was stronger than any storm she had ever experienced. Prayers for him continued, sometimes in a fervent whisper and at others in a railing cyclone of rage. She careened on the edge of a tantrum at any given moment, then at other times, a calm resolve of understanding overcame her that One greater and more powerful than she, was at the helm of her life. Her emotions were tossed up and down as if on waves on the ocean. Caught up in a whirlpool of questions of his well-being, she was ready to drown.

"Prudence, you seem far away. Are you all right?"

"Sorry, Mother. I'm fine."

"You haven't eaten a bite. The soup you are swirling around almost sloshed out of the bowl."

Prudence looked down at the spoon in her hand as if seeing it for the first time. Her bowl showed signs the soup indeed almost left the confines. "I am in turmoil like I cause this soup."

"Do you want to talk about it?"

"A letter from Oliver would solve most of my anxiety."

"I understand. Our men are in a dangerous place and we have not heard a word."

"I'm sorry, Mama. I shouldn't have mentioned it. You are missing Father as much as or more so than I miss Oliver."

Granny placed her hand over Prudence's. "It never gets easier. Only different. I lost your grandfather fifteen years ago and I miss him as much today as I did then. I talk to him every day. He is still with me but in a different way. My heavenly Father comforts me when the missing gets rough. Do you talk to Oliver? Write him letters you keep until you can give them to him personally?"

Prudence scrutinized the wisdom in her grandmother's soft blue eyes and traced a few of the myriad of wrinkles that years of life well lived had wrought. Wisdom and strength exuded from this woman before her. She needed to take heed.

Her mother and grandmother were strong, God-fearing wives and mothers who had learned the lessons of life that the Lord had given them. They were under no delusion they had learned it all. Prudence would lean in and pull from their deep well.

"Have faith. Not only in God but in His wisdom and right hand that holds Oliver and loves him more than you do," Granny said.

Auntie said, "If Oliver doesn't make it home, you will survive."

"Emeline. Please use good thoughts. Cheerful encouraging thoughts," Mother said.

Later in the quiet of her room, those words from her mother and grandmother echoed in Prudence's mind. She wanted to believe and come out of this a strong woman. She got ready for bed and burrowed into the softness. A drowsiness came over her. The words of encouragement from earlier swirled around her head. Then another voice crowded in. *"If Oliver doesn't make it home, you will survive."*

"No!" She sat straight up. "No." She couldn't think those thoughts. They would destroy her.

Chapter 12

Oliver leaned closer to catch the words being said by the men at the table a few feet away. Not to let them know he listened, he fiddled with his boot. Secrets. He dealt in secrets. He lived a secret. Listened to secrets. Put secrets into codes and passed them on and decoded others. Invisible ink held other secrets. Hidden compartments guarded scraps of paper filled with more secrets.

Some would call him a patriot spy—others, a traitor to the crown. He did what he did because he believed in the cause and followed orders and was good at his job. The red coat he sometimes wore made him feel a traitor. The disguises he donned made his head swim. Wigs itched and clothing never quite fit. What would his beloved Prudence think?

He refocused his mind on the task at hand. The mumbled words he imprinted on his memory. The men stood and left. The battle within to fight the impulse to follow bound him tighter than a cat ready to pounce on a mouse.

At his elbow he heard a familiar voice say, "Always nursing the same ale but never buying a man a drink. Some might think you're here for other matters. Come with me. Now." The man left.

Oliver turned to make sure and scanned the room again. He swallowed the rest of his drink, slowly stood, and nonchalantly walked to the back door. The short distance, only a few blocks, kept his senses active to determine he wasn't followed.

In a dark alley, he opened a door and slipped into a dim room. A burlap bag fell over his head and his arms were jerked behind and bound. "Don't make a sound," an unfamiliar voice said.

All of Oliver's senses went into full alert. Questions screamed inside his brain. Who? Why? What? Was his cover blown? How did he allow this to happen?

Slammed into a chair, Oliver winced.

"We will sit tight for a while until it gets nice and dark. Relax. We won't kill you. Time and the British will do that for us." An evil laugh followed.

Another voice chimed in, echoing the laugh.

The burlap tickled and roughened his face and neck. "What do you want with me?"

No answer.

"Money? Release me and I'll hand—"

"We get paid when we deliver you. Now shut your mouth." Time passed. The voices whispered. Oliver sat like a statue and strained to listen and record snippets of information and odors, anything to help him know who his abductors were. A door opened and a whoosh of air met him. "Time to go for a little journey."

"Where?"

"Never you mind. Remember, I might as well hand you over dead as alive. Keep quiet."

Hands jerked him up and guided him out the room. He shuffled, not knowing where to place his feet.

"Keep moving. Don't try anything." Something dug into his ribs, probably a pistol.

The ground under him changed. Cobblestones. The street. If only he knew where they were taking him. They walked for, he guessed, five minutes.

Oliver was half-dragged down stone steps. Salty sea smell hit his nose. A seagull called. Another answered. He detected water splashing. Against what? A pier? A boat?

"Lift your leg. Into the skiff you go." A push and he landed hard on the surface. The rocking indicated he boarded a small sea vessel. He sat. A hand clamped on his shoulder preventing him from rising. "A short ride and then the Brits will deal with you." Again the pistol prodded his ribs.

He felt the boat move silently through the water. They must be paddling. After a while, the boat slid to thump against maybe a hull of a larger ship. Someone helped him to his feet, unbound his hands, and placed them on a rope. His head still covered, they picked up his leg and set his foot on a rung. "Climb."

Carefully, with every bit of awareness of what a missed step could bring, he inched upward. Not knowing the exact placement of the water, he rethought his impulse to jump and instead obeyed. "Don't try anything. My man has his pistol pointed at your back."

Oliver must have reached the top, for hands tugged him in and righted him. He was pulled away from the slapping of the water. Again shoved into a chair. A door closed. He waited. Not a noise. He moved his hands and no one stopped him. He whipped off the hood. He blinked in the light. Across the room sat a British sea captain.

"You have been a very busy man. A traitor to the Crown and punishable by hanging. Cooperate and we might go lenient. Instead of swinging, you'd wear irons in the hold. A good trade. Your life for information."

"I don't know what you are referring to." Oliver looked around the captain's quarters. "Your men mistakenly grabbed the wrong man. I'm a soldier in the King's army."

"You are wearing our uniform but I am quite apprised of your true operandi."

The door opened. A uniformed man entered. "Captain?"

"Yes, take him below. A stint there will undoubtedly loosen his tongue. Please unburden him of the uniform."

"Stand up."

Oliver complied.

"Turn around."

He obeyed. Shackles were clamped on his wrists. The officer led him out and to the trapdoor to the hold. The man stomped twice on the door and it opened. A head poked out.

"You have a new resident. Bring back his uniform."

Oliver was shoved.

"Go on."

Oliver had no choice but to comply. He turned, bent, and stepped onto the top of the ladder. He took hold of the ladder and descended a number of steps into the dark abyss. The stench overwhelmed him. He gagged. Coughed.

"You'll get used to it."

At the bottom the man said, "Come with me. I have a place all ready for you."

He brought his arm up to breathe through his coat and followed the man clothed in dirty garments who hadn't seen a bath is some time. Rodents scurried freely about the sacks and crates. The dim lamps hung infrequently giving off an eerie glow. Insects swarmed him and he swiped them away to no avail. He passed men in all degrees of health. Some curled in corners, appeared to be near death, moaning and cursing while other heaps were silent, perhaps already death had captured their souls.

A three-sided cage backed to the hull awaited him. The guard took off his handcuffs. "Take off your clothes. And put this on." Filthy rags were thrust at him.

Oliver undressed and redressed in the disease-ridden clothes, probably stripped off a corpse before the body was tossed into the sea.

"Get in."

Oliver stepped into the cage. The clang of the door brought him to swivel back as the key turned in the lock. Almost silent footfalls of the man faded away. His new quarters were roughly five feet by five feet. Too small for him to stretch out. The height, to the deck above. No window could be seen anywhere. His eyes penetrated the darkness. A bucket stood in the corner for his necessary use.

"My God. Where are You?"

"There is no God in this hold," came the reply.

Oliver turned to squint in the gloom into the cage beside him and what he had thought a pile of rags emerged a pale grimy face.

Chapter 13

Prudence felt her world as unsteady as a mudslide. An eternity it seemed since Jonas reluctantly handed her the letter from Oliver. The reply from the Committee of Safety did not exactly help her the way she had anticipated.

We regret to inform you that although a worthy cause to intervene on your behalf, we are shorthanded at present with all our men occupied with the war. When we beat our oppressors there will be no need for us to help, as these aggressors will be vanquished.

God's speed.

A promise of interaction from the Committee had kept Cox at bay. But with this answer, how much longer could she forestall his threats and sign the land over?

A few months ago, Jonas had started making bolder advances. More and more frequently, he visited or appeared where she worked in the fields. Even with others around, he still persisted. A call to Brutus always brought Jonas up short and made him keep his distance. How the dog detected a need to protect her from him was a mystery.

"Lovely Prudence," Jonas called out one morning as she alone checked the progress of the wheat. Lost in her inspection she had not detected his approach.

She straightened. "Jonas."

"Have you received a letter from Oliver?"

"No." She shook her head.

"Nothing could stop me from finding a way to get word to the woman I loved. Of course I'd never leave one so fair alone. Have you considered he is not able to write? Injured? Captured? Or worse."

"Jonas, please. Don't be cruel."

"Come away with me." He stepped closer and reached out his hand.

"Brutus!"

The dog raced out from behind the rows and stopped beside her. A low growl came from his throat.

"Easy, boy. You know me."

Prudence lifted her eyebrow. "I'm afraid he does. Now, if you will leave my property."

He took a few steps backwards. "Prudence. A woman like you shouldn't work the fields. Nor should you be alone. Prude, don't be coy, you want comfort as much as I. Bread, cheese, and a bottle of wine. I've saved some hidden away for a special occasion." He lowered his voice. "Come anytime. My door is always open for you." He jumped up onto his horse. "Anytime."

She didn't move until he had gone from sight. "Good boy, Brutus. I'm sure he is just taunting me. Thank you for showing him that you would step in to protect me. Let's go home."

A few days later, Silas came into the parlor, where the ladies were enjoying each other's company, with a note.

"This arrived a bit ago. Addressed to Miss Prudence Ainsworth." He handed the page to her.

She unfolded the paper and read,

My dear Miss Ainsworth. I come tomorrow at noon to receive an answer to my proposition. The request has changed. No more will I only take the parcel of land but your hand in marriage as well. I will be accompanied by a priest and my associates in red. My friends in high places stated that there will not be any so called help from your precious Committee.

I got a dispatch today detailing the demise of one Oliver Duke.

"No!" Prudence screamed and buried her head in her hands with sobs. The letter, discarded, floated to the floor. Her mother rushed over and took her in her arms. "Whatever did it say?"

Auntie picked up the letter and read aloud, finishing with:

Wear the pretty gown I know you made a few years ago for your wedding. The dress is delicate and soft and I'm sure still fits you quite nicely. I want my bride looking ravishing. We will consummate our vows at my house for privacy reasons but you may pick your house or mine for our residence.

Remember, noon. Don't disappoint or your family will be banned and house torched.
Archibald Cox

Spirited away by Granny, accompanied by Brutus and Gafton, Prudence wanted to melt into a puddle of self-pity. Instead, she rode silently through the darkness. "Where are we going?" asked a sleepy young voice riding in front of her, huddled under her cloak.

"Granny has a plan. We are going on an adventure. Gafton, do you like stories? I'll tell you one when we reach our destination."

The boy settled against her. She followed her Granny deeper into the forest. The horses picked their way by the light of the moon. No discernable path could be seen.

Quite a while later, they came upon a small, dark cabin. Prudence detected a whiff of smoke coming from the chimney. "Where are we?"

"Friends of mine."

They dismounted. "Brutus, stay." Prudence said and patted the dog's head.

Granny walked up to the front door and knocked. "It's me, Keziah."

The door opened spilling a sliver of light across the threshold. "Come."

Granny held Gafton's hand as she entered. Prudence followed and the door closed behind her. A small, older Indian woman stood behind her. Prudence smiled at her and surveyed the interior of the cabin. The room in which they entered held a rug, a few pieces of furniture, stove, and a fireplace. Although sparse, the space was welcoming and homey.

A man rose from a chair beside the fireplace. "Welcome, Keziah. It's been a long time. Come, sit. Tell me what brings you."

Granny took off her cloak. "Prudence, it's all right now. Please relax." She walked forward and said, "Hassun, this is my granddaughter, Prudence. Prudence, Hassun."

Prudence bowed. "Nice to meet you."

Granny turned to the woman who let them in. "Kimi, I'd like to introduce you to my granddaughter, Prudence. Prudence, Kimi, my dear friend."

Prudence dipped her head. "It's wonderful to meet one of Granny's friends."

Granny put her arm around Gafton. "This is one we call our own. Gafton. He is a strong worker and helper."

Prudence, Granny, and Gafton sat on the rug near the fire. Granny spoke of the upcoming marriage between Prudence and Oliver, Oliver's silence, and the threat from Cox. The Nanticoke couple listened with grave expressions.

"Please stay as long as you need. We have room and plenty of food to spare. We welcome you."

"Thank you." Prudence marveled at their seemly natural use of her native tongue. "My dog is out front and used to my proximity. Will he be a problem?"

Kimi went to the door and pulled it open. She

whistled and the dog ran in and straight to Prudence to flop down and place his head on her lap.

Granny rose. "I must return tonight, so I do not show anyone watching where I came from. Brutus stays here."

"Granny, I fear for you to go alone," said Prudence.

Hassun stood. "I will go with you."

Prudence hugged Granny and tears slid down her face. "I feel as if I'm losing you too."

"Child." Granny cupped Prudence's cheek. "You can't lose me. I'll always be here." She pointed to Prudence's heart. "Oliver, your father, mother, and Auntie are all with you. Most importantly, your heavenly Father is with you. He hasn't given up on you. Trust Him to get you through this difficult time."

"Do you truly believe Cox told me a lie and Oliver is still alive?"

"My dear Prudence, what does your heart tell you? Have you prayed about all of this?"

Prudence didn't answer.

Granny gathered her in her arms one more time and then she and Hassun left.

Chapter 14

Oliver slept fitfully in a sitting position. Unable to stretch out. Six days had passed, if he counted correctly. When not trying to sleep, he paced. A difficult occupation given the cramped space. He used the bars to pull himself off the floor over and over to keep his muscles strong.

Questions bombarded his mind. Why did he end up here? How did it happen? In the tavern, his contact told him to follow but when he got to their designated location he had been apprehended. Did his contact turn? If so, how many others had gone missing? Did he get ambushed also?

Food and water were scarce. Although served disgusting gruel, a man needed to consume the slop before critters ascended. A fight with a rat the size of his thigh and teeth sharper than knives would not be enjoyable. This place was a stink hole. He counted four dead since he arrived. Every day gone by made survival a bit dimmer, catapulting the need to get out of here to the stars.

Oliver had not been summoned by the captain. Had he been forgotten? What of Prudence and his family? Did they mourn him, thinking he died? To keep them safe, he had not communicated since he saw Jonas. Did Jonas deliver the letter? Tell Mother about him? How much time had passed since he handed the letter to Jonas? Two and a half years? Far too long. Poor, sweet Prudence. Would she wait? Did she give up hope of ever seeing him again?

The questions and worry might tear him apart. Despair certainly would! No, he would not let despair creep in. He knew God loved him and held everything in His hand. No time like the present to pray and reach out to the One who gave peace.

He knelt and bowed his head. Deep in his prayer, he lost time and himself. His focus turned toward the Lord and his trust and faith were restored.

A key scraped in the lock. He startled and looked up. His keeper motioned for him to follow.

Oliver stood and did as he was bid, weaving through the maze the way they had entered a lifetime ago. His guide stopped. "Go above."

Up the ladder to the top. Hand up to protect his eyes, he squinted. His eyes burned and tears formed. The sun bright in the sky was unbearable for a moment. Slowly, he could take the light. An officer approached. "The captain is expecting you, but a bath first."

A bath would be welcome. He followed to the

side of the ship. The ship sat in a large harbor where other ships floated with the British flag. The officer stopped before a metal cage. "Step in."

Oliver started to ask, "Wha…" A gun stock was thrust into his gut. He gasped and bent over. This time he moved in when told to.

The officer closed and locked the cage. "Now!"

A creaking sound and his cage shifted. Up with a jolt a fraction of a time. He realized men pulled ropes and chains to hoist him up. Why he did not know. *Would they bake him in the sun?*

High above deck, the cage swiveled out over the ocean. Unbelievably, they lowered the cage with Oliver inside to the ocean! A splash and he broke the surface. His feet got wet. The water—cold. The water inched up his calves. Thighs. Stomach. How far down would they take him? His chest. Shoulders. Instinct tilted his chin up. Water in his ears. *Merciful Lord!*

A huge breath and his head went under.

Prudence cried herself to sleep. Weeks went by and Granny had not come back for her. A cloud of despair descended. A listlessness came over her. She hardly ate. Brutus frequently placed his head on her lap and whined.

Hassun told her when he came back from taking her Granny, "Your grandmother safe at her home. Your mother sends love and says you pray."

For years she received no news from Oliver and now she was cut off from her family too. The fight in her faded. Prudence couldn't dredge up the willpower needed.

Hassun and Kimi were gracious and kind and made Prudence feel welcome and cared for. Gafton seemed to enjoy this season. Hassun spent time with him. The boy thrived under a man's tutelage and guidance. Gafton clung unto every word and action the tall man did—whether learning to sharpen tools or spear, or listening to tales of their people.

Prudence needed to be strong for Gafton's sake. A difficult task. The energy it took to care for him depleted her of the strength to do other tasks. His young eyes had seen enough heartache. After she knew he slept, she allowed the tears to fall. Every night.

One morning, Kimi asked, "Prudence, will you come walk with me?"

Prudence agreed. She left Gafton in Hassun's care but took Brutus with her. The cabin sat in a small clearing in the thick forest. Kimi led them on a narrow trail. "Deer trail. They are used to my scent. We hunt far from here and only for food and skins. Deer are majestic creatures. We respect them.

"There are others who do not. They hunt not for food but for profit. Fox, beaver, bear, wolf, deer, raccoon, and large birds. They sell pelts, skins, and feathers, and discard most of the meat. What a waste." Kimi shook her head.

"I came upon a fawn in a fox trap. She fought me, making her injuries worse. I spoke quiet and sang soothing songs. Still she fought. She did not trust me. After hours, in exhaustion she finally let me release her. I had slipped a rope around her neck so I could fix her wound. Again the fight. At the end of both of our strength she let me lead her home where I nursed her. Fearful of me at first. I fed her. Bathed and wrapped the wound. Every day she became less afraid. Her trust in me grew. She got strong. Healed. I took her back in the deep woods to set her free. Unsure now of her natural environment, she shook and trembled. Fear grabbed her again. She followed me home. I had become her mother, protection, a source of food, and security."

"What became of her?"

"She is following us."

Prudence turned where Kimi pointed. There stood a beautiful graceful doe, not far away. Her eyes were on Kimi. Her posture alert.

"Oh. Is she always near you?"

"Yes. Sadly, she is. Strong and healed yet still afraid and unsure. She does not trust who she is—a deer to run and frolic, mate and have babies. You are like that doe."

"What do you mean?"

"You are strong and whole. Yet afraid and unsure. You do not fully trust your world. Your God. Trust Him. You have deep fear. Fear for the life of those you love. Too afraid to trust the One who is in control. The One to help you through the times ahead and heal you."

"When did you learn of my God?"

"Hassun and I do not live with our people because we found your God. Years ago, white man told us. Our people shun us."

"I'm so sorry. I didn't know. You both seem content. Happy."

"We are. We trust God who made the world. We choose Him knowing what would happen. Do you trust Him with everything?"

"Yes."

"With Oliver? Your mother? Father? Grandmother? Your house and lands?"

Prudence looked at the ground. "I'm not sure."

"Make sure. I leave you now. This path will take you farther to a river and back to our home. Brutus, I'm sure, can find the way if you get lost. Just stay on trail." She pointed to the skinny track. "Go. Talk to God."

Prudence watched the wise woman silently walk back the way they had come. The doe followed. She and Brutus were alone.

Chapter 15

Wallabout Bay,
Brooklyn New York
1783

Oliver shivered in the belly of the ship. Drenched and cold. He had lived through another dunking. The last time his lungs almost exploded. Fire burned in them as the men finally brought him to the surface. The water was ice cold. About to pass out, he broke the surface to laughter. The men's sport at his expense. A form of torture. Through all that, and all these days, he still had not talked to the captain. The captain stood up by the helm, apparently overseeing his crew almost drown him.

He readied himself for the next time. He had a plan. He'd kept and sharpened scraps of bone along the rough rusty cage bars. He mumbled, "A long narrow sliver ought to do the trick."

"Don't think ye can escape. Me legs got broke for me trouble." Patty spoke from his corner next to Oliver's cage.

"A man's got to try." Oliver didn't expect the man to reply. His words were scarce and only above a whisper.

Sparse sleep and only a bit of exercise and not adequate food—he hoped he would be strong enough.

Days later, the guard came for him. He slowly followed, gearing up for what he would attempt. He had one try. Again the sun attacked his eyes. Head bowed, he shuffled forward to the target. No need to let on his strength and determination.

Inside the cage, he descended into the murky water. Waves lapped against the ship. *Dear Lord, I need help.*

A clap of thunder! Rain drops. Gradually they let him down, dipping deeper into the cold water.

The rain fell in earnest. The men's laughter was almost undetectable. They didn't stop his progress into the depths. Half in and half out of the water, they plunged him lower. As soon as he felt confident they would not see what he did, he slid the bone from his sleeve. He knew from trying it out that his hands fit between the bars. He inserted the bone into the lock and twisted and wiggled it. He caught the biggest breath of his life just before his head went under. They took him farther down than other times. Good. The lock opened. Now to push with all his strength. A difficult task with not much to brace against.

His body slipped through the opening into the

open bay. He kicked off the bars away from the ship. His lungs burned. Still under, he let out a bit more air.

He needed a breath! *Lord!* He broke the surface and gasped. Rain beat the water. Down he went. Swam. Up for another breath. Rain and waves met him. He sputtered. Oliver gazed around to get his bearings. A storm had come from nowhere covering his progress. *Thank the Lord!* Which way to go?

Prudence had never before looked deep in her heart. She peeled and poked. Asked herself questions. As her prayers changed, she changed. The flimsy veneer she had built of protection, a mock confidence and pride in herself, melted away. Piece by piece, she replaced it with a true confidence and assurance in God. A sliver of hope in a future that only the Lord could give, started to sprout. Why did it hurt, yet feel so good? Tears streamed. Peace cascaded down from on high. A new resolve to let go and trust came from deep within.

She trusted Providence. He had control of her life, her loved ones, even Oliver. She released the grip she held over her love of Oliver and gave him to her mighty Lord. Prudence felt light as if she could float to the dwelling of the Most High.

The sun had almost disappeared. "Brutus, we need to go back." She rested her hand on his head as they picked their way, with her feet on the scarce path and his in the brush. The dimness didn't seem to bother him.

The forest opened up to the clearing and the

comforting sight of the cabin. Another horse stood tied to a tree, grazing. "Granny!"

Prudence ran. Brutus beside her. She flung open the door. Granny took her in an embrace and the tears started again.

"My dear child. No, I didn't come with news from Oliver."

Over supper, Granny filled her in on the events of the past months. The three women, the help, and the plantation were right as rain. Cox's friends hadn't stayed. "They seemed to have no stomach to bother with a few old women." She laughed. "When you weren't there, they got wise to what Cox had cooked up. Their allegiance had declined. I'd imagine our weapons added to their unease. Your wise mother mentioned correspondence with the Safety Committee and they all but raced to their horses to hasten away."

Her granny had a huge grin. "Mr. Cox had no recourse but to leave."

"But the Committee said they couldn't help us."

"Yes, but your mother didn't refer to the content of their letter—only that we had received one. A higher power directed that encounter. We made the right decision bringing you and Gafton here for a while." Granny ruffled his hair. He grinned and leaned against her. "I waited a time to make sure the man didn't do anything stupid or bother us. The next is the most important news."

"What could be more important than all you said?"

"The war is over! We can breathe again."

"Did I hear correctly?"

Granny nodded. "Yes, my girl. Our loved ones will be on their way home. Soon."

"Any word?"

"Your father is safe and must be en route. I'm sorry, still no news from Oliver."

Prudence smiled even though her heart quaked. Trusting was difficult. Questions still plagued her. What if Oliver didn't want her after all this time? Had he changed? Did he fight the demons in his life as she had with hers? She squared her shoulders. "I'm so pleased. Father will be home soon. God will take care of him. Oliver is in His hands as well. I just need to trust."

Granny hugged her. "That's my girl."

Prudence spoke to them about her solitude with her Heavenly Father. Unshed tears pooled in her granny's eyes and Hassun and Kimi smiled knowing smiles. Gafton listened with wide eyes as if understanding the ordeal. Who knew a child's perception and what this particular child had gone through?

In the morning Prudence sat Gafton on the saddle of Hautboy and climbed up behind. Anticipation filled her. She couldn't wait to hug her mother and prayed her father and Oliver would be waiting. One only needed to demonstrate faith.

Oliver lay on the shore, panting. Rain had let up and a foggy drizzle banked the shore. Under cover of clouds, he rose. Oliver didn't know exactly where he had come ashore. Might it be near the town where he lived and frequented the local establishments? He shivered. The chill in the air made him realize, the seasons turned from summer to fall. Food. Water. Clothes. He clicked off his immediate needs. His body quaked. Clothes and shelter came to the top of his list. What direction should he go? Oliver headed out, hoping to easily procure his list for survival.

Haste lest he be recaptured, but cautious. A battle of both waged in his being. In the shadows and crevices, behind objects, he made his way inland as quickly as possible. His spy mind worked at how and what would be his next move.

A persuader at his core, he concocted many tales to weave to get everything. Stealing was stealing but in war… He memorized the addresses to later send money to replace the borrowed items. First things first. A few articles at different locations to not point to a thief.

He borrowed a razor and shaved his face and head to rid him of lice. A fast bath with lye soap did the rest.

Once he had donned clean dry clothes a bit too large and had a full stomach, he needed to find a place secure where he could sleep. Out a few miles from town, he found a barn and hid in the hay.

Chapter 16

Dead. Prudence's dreams were shattered.

Christmas had always been her favorite time of year. At age five, their decorated Christmas tree held a beautiful glass ornament which above all others attracted her attention.

"Don't touch. Just look," were the words of her wise mother.

The sunlight from the window sparkled off the round orb, drawing her to lift the bauble from the secure branch. She held it up to the light, sending swirls of sparkles glistening around the room. The ball bore a painted picture of the nativity on one side and the other side a whirling array of different colors. Prudence spun the ornament, creating a cascade of brilliant rainbows to shimmer across the ceiling. That's when it happened. The beautiful creation slipped from her grasp and crashed to the floor.

The shattered mess caused Prudence to drop on her knees in anguished cries. She had been warned. Her punishment had been the devastation of breaking such exquisite beauty. Tears streamed down her chubby cheeks as she watched the shards being swept away.

Now, a sob caught in her throat as she remembered the tragic event which heightened the feelings of despair. Her dreams of a life with Oliver shattered like the delicate ornament had years ago. What would she do?

Over three months since the end of the war and still no letter from Oliver. Could he not get home? His silence pointed to an injury so great he couldn't write or he had been captured and not released by the British or Hessians. The other alternative was too horrible to even think about.

The dream of being together seemed unattainable. Doubt and despair's ugly tentacles started at the edge of her heart.

Her resolve to trust quaked and threatened to crumble. No! She would not fall into the pit of wretchedness.

Prudence turned her thoughts to joyful things. Her father made it home safe. Injured but safe. He lost toes to frostbite and would forever limp. Alive—that was the most important thing. The family would celebrate Christmas soon. A happy celebration now that the war was over and they had a child in the house. The delightful addition to their family, Gafton, brought smiles from everyone including Auntie. Her father had taken to him and the boy followed him around like a puppy followed its mother.

Prudence moved the lit candelabra to the center of the table and swiped at invisible dust. More light was needed to dispel the dark of the night. An evening Christmas party might bring a cheer to this sad heart of hers. Her mother and father wanted a simple celebration with friends who had weathered the terrible war. She went along even though her heart felt heavy. Her emotions were up and down, like the bucket tied to a rope that one of the maids used to gather water from the well. One minute she trusted completely and had peace, expecting Oliver to walk in the door any moment. The next, she sank and would need to pull herself back up.

A party. Prudence squared her shoulders and said a little prayer. Her eyes traveled to the Christmas tree. A smile played at the corners of her mouth as she pictured Gafton's delight when he helped them decorate. She enlisted the boy's help to gather the stored decorations and he confided that his family had never celebrated. Christmas celebrations were not as popular when Prudence was a child but had gained in popularity as she grew older. Of course a joyful Christmas was what everyone needed. Focusing on the birth of the Lord was a celebration indeed.

Brutus pulled on Prudence's skirts, bringing her out of her reverie. "Not now, boy. I don't have time to play. Guests are arriving and you should be tied outside." Brutus's persistence was uncharacteristic. He whipped his body and therefore her dress around, almost tearing the satin. She flung the way he tugged. She grabbed the table to steady herself. Her eye caught a reflection in the glass of the window. Prudence blinked. The reflection in glass didn't fade. "No! It can't be!" She spun the other way. "Brutus! Release!" The dog let go and led her to what she had dreamed of seeing for the last eight long years. Her legs almost buckled. She staggered and then flew to his waiting arms.

"Oh, my sweet Oliver! You're alive!" His arms were around her and her tears poured unbidden.

"I told you I'd come back," he whispered in her ear.

Giddy with delight, she desired he should lift her on his steed and speed her away because this dream might fade as hers had done when she woke each morning.

"I am here, my darling. I've yearned to hold you all these past years. I will never leave you again."

"Oh, Oliver."

Disregarding propriety, his lips came down on hers. Passion erupted.

"Now the party can officially start," her father said and clamped Oliver on his shoulder.

The couple jerked apart. Oliver slid his hand down to capture hers in a tight grip. He turned toward her father, never letting her go of her hand. "Sir. I see you came home."

"I did. I perceive you had a terrible time getting here."

"Yes, sir." He wiped his hand down his shirt. "You'll have to forgive my undress. I didn't go home but came straight here."

"Do not worry. We are relieved you are home. Although, I'm afraid we are about to be inundated with company. A Christmas party."

Prudence pinched herself. She winced. Awake. Relief swept over her.

Brutus clambered for attention.

Oliver bent and ruffled his fur. "Are you pleased to see me, boy? Thank you for taking care of my dear Prudence."

People started to arrive. Oliver pulled her away through the halls to her father's office. "Prudence, say something."

"You're alive! Kiss me again!"

He took her into his arms. The kiss lingered but a little less fiery this time. The same as her memory. Those dreams were not as sweet as the real thing.

He had lost weight. So had she. They were together and that was what mattered.

Music floated in. "Can I have the pleasure of this dance?" She grinned and he led her in a minuet. Their feet remembered the moves. Prudence gazed in his eyes.

His look intensified. "Will you marry me?"

"Always, anytime, anywhere. Is tonight too soon?"

He laughed and danced her back with the others to find her father.

The whispers and swift movement of her friends, family, and staff reminded her of bees around the rose bushes in spring. In a little over an hour the Christmas party became a bridal ceremony.

Prudence was whisked upstairs away from Oliver. Auntie took a few tucks into her saved wedding dress to make it fit like it did before the war.

"You are beautiful." Her mother pulled her into an embrace.

Her father kissed her cheek and said, "I am the proudest man alive. I'm privileged to oversee your vows and pronounce you married tonight."

Granny hugged her. "A fine, fair girl. A woman who learned to trust. You may have lost weight but you grew wisdom and strength these past years."

"Thank you, Granny."

The family left her to hurry down to await her descent.

Oliver returned with his best clothes on, though loose, he felt better dressed than he had in years.

His mother almost fainted when he had arrived home. "Oliver! I thought you were dead! Are you a spirit or alive?"

He kissed her worried brow. "I'm getting married. Hurry and change. Where is Jonas?"

"He left a mere hour ago. All of a sudden. He acted like snakes were after him."

Oliver rifled through his brother's room searching for the third ring in the gimmal set for Prudence. To no avail. Disappointed but not disheartened, he prepared for the ceremony he had anticipated and fought to live for so it might happen.

Now, standing in front of the windows in the great hall at Ainsworth Plantation, Oliver waited for his love to meet him. On one side sat Brutus and on the other, his future father-in-law stood beside him.

Musicians played. People perched on rows of chairs impatient for Prudence appear.

A hush ascended. Prudence entered. He caught his breath. Amazingly lovely. None to compare to his beautiful bride. His heart skipped a beat. His eyes found hers. She gracefully floated toward him.

Soon her hand rested in his and they faced her father.

Oliver's voice rang out strong in response to Reverend Ainsworth's directive. "I promise to love and cherish you, dear Prudence. To provide for you and comfort you in distress. To lead you with understanding and cultivate joy in our union."

"Oliver, I vow to respect you as the head of our family. To work alongside you and be your helper. I promise to do my best to give you children. And to bring no shame to your family name."

Her father said, "Oliver, do you present a ring as a symbol of your vows?"

"Yes. Prudence wears one. I wear the other." Oliver took off his ring and slid it onto her gloved finger. "Unfortunately, my brother…"

"Your brother is late. I carry the third," Jonas said from the back of the room. Oliver and Prudence turned. Brutus stood.

"Prudence said, "It's all right, Brutus." She placed her hand on the broad head.

Jonas strode to them. He handed the ring to Oliver. "Dear brother, I wanted to run away when I saw you had returned. Lately, and because I had a scrape with a few of the wrong sort, I've come to see myself as others might. I've been deplorable and I want to apologize to you and your bride." He dipped his head toward Prudence. "Please forgive me. I've been prideful and arrogant. And smeared our good name. I will henceforth live an upright life." He peered over his shoulder. A beautiful woman stood just outside the doorway. She smiled her encouragement. Jonas turned back and continued, "Hannah has helped me become a gentleman. I'm determined to honor her and bring back my good name. Also, I must say, Prudence should be commended for being true, strong, and determined."

"What are you talking about?"

"This is not the time. Please carry on." He nodded to her father, turned, and walked back to take Hannah by the hand and brought her to where they could join his parents.

Her father cleared his throat. "Oliver, continue with the rings."

Oliver nodded. "Prudence, this last ring binds the other two together." He twisted the ring he had slid onto her finger and it wedged into place. The three rings were bound.

Her father said, "Oliver and Prudence, as these three rings became one, symbolizing God, Man, and Wife, under God Almighty's watchful eye, I give you each other and pronounce you husband and wife and no man may break this union.

"Oliver, you may kiss your bride."

The kiss Oliver gave her, although chaste, was full of promise.

The happy couple left the hall arm in arm and fled in a carriage already packed for their adventure. He knew of a place they might spend the night and travel on from there. "Dear, come spring, I want to take you to a peaceful stream where so long ago I envisioned a walk with you, my lovely Prudence. I sat on a rock beside the water and penned a letter and sent it in Jonas's hand to you. Too bad the other letters I penned and kept were lost."

Oliver shook his head then smiled. "Every day on our trip, I plan on whispering them from my memory to you." He leaned over and gave her a deep kiss and a thrill raced through him as she reciprocated with passion.

Out of breath, he ended the kiss.

Oliver smiled and traced his finger down her cheek. "So beautiful. I will never get tired of gazing at your face. The real thing replaces the one I stored in my head."

"I, too, want to behold you every moment of every day. We were separated to the point of despair. I thank the Lord for bringing us back together and in one piece. I also wrote words of love in letters that I'll share with you." Prudence pulled a box from her satchel. "I kept the ones from you and added my own. Never knowing where you were, or who to send them with, I didn't try." She opened the wooden box, revealing pages upon pages stuffed in the interior.

Prudence lifted her eyes to his. "Please tell me of all you encountered, both the good and the bad. I want to know where you traveled and things you endured. I feel you have changed. Grown stronger. So many questions can now be answered."

"I perceive a new wisdom in the depth of your eyes." He cradled her head and kissed the furrow between her eyes. "We have so much to catch up on."

"A lifetime we have lived, and yet we are given a lifetime still to live, my love." She snuggled under his free arm as he drove the carriage to their destination to start their long full life together.

The End

Reviews

I hope you enjoyed **Reflection in Glass.** I loved creating this romantic suspense.
If you enjoyed this tale, please write a review on Amazon and Goodreads.
Reviews are the writer's lifeblood. Readers and authors love to read reviews.
Your review doesn't need to be long. A few words goes a long way.
To review this book, catch me on my author pages:
https://www.amazon.com/Robin-Densmore-Fuson/e/B06XGKVDDV/ref

https://www.goodreads.com/author/show/6604786.Robin_Densmore_Fuson

Thank you!

Other Books by the Author

Historical:
The Dress shop
Lasso Love
Gamble on Fate

Contemporary:
Etching in the Snow
A Sparkle of Silver

Children's books:
Rosita Valdez and the Giant Sea Turtle
Rosita Valdez and the Attic's Secret
Rosita Valdez and the Spanish Doll

https://www.amazon.com/Robin-Densmore-Fuson/e/B06XGKVDDV/ref

For your pleasure included in the next few pages are a few chapters of *Gamble on Fate* a historical fiction with a bit of a twist.

Gamble on Fate
Colorado Territory 1868
(Near present day Colorado Springs, Colorado)

Chapter 1

A rifle shot! The stagecoach lurched forward and picked up speed.

Lydia poked her head out the side window. No sign of the driver. The horses were galloping at a high rate of speed. She wriggled through the narrow opening, grabbed the luggage rack on the roof, and started for the top. Her feet slipped off the window frame. "Aahh!"

A hand snatched her ankle and placed her foot firmly on the frame. She barely took time to acknowledge. Her flailing foot joined the other and she caught a steadying breath.

The ascent up the side proved difficult as wind whipped her hair and skirts, trying to dislodge her. She tightened her grip. The hat was long gone. No footholds could be found but the rail on the crown of the coach. At a crazy angle her right foot found the top as she hung on and pulled up. The out-of-control horses pounded the ground in a frenzy to get away from an unknown assailant.

A mound of suitcases on top caused more difficulty to her maneuvers. The jolting of the coach made her teeth rattle, causing her to clinch her jaw. She risked a look over the side. A face peered at her out of the window she had vacated. Lydia prostrated her body face down and inched toward the front. She peered over the edge of the carriage to ascertain the situation. Blood poured from a bullet wound in the shoulder of the slumped driver. The angle of his head indicated he may have knocked himself out. Dead?

Horse reins flapped on the ground. The team of six horses had no guidance except themselves. In the process of descending to the seat, the horses swerved, causing her to tumble onto the injured man. He moaned but didn't move. Alive!

The reins were a problem. She needed them to gain control of this vehicle. With one hand clasped on the footrest, she reached down. Jolted along, Lydia kept missing the wildly swaying leather and caught only air. The ground sped beneath them. The horses needed to be stopped.

She scrambled and stood to grab the rack on the top of the coach to steady herself as she tugged the hem of her skirt up and into her belt. Perspiration soaked her shirtwaist.

Lydia closed her eyes for a brief silent prayer. In petticoats and drawers she leapt onto the left horse of the closest team. After a moment to stabilize and catch the galloping rhythm, she jumped to the next. Her heart pounded as she watched the ground fly past. The horses' hooves thundered. Another deep breath and leap landed her on the left horse on the leading team. She took the harness reins on the bridle and pulled back.

The horses didn't heed nor slow. She had to reach over and grab the reins on her right. Her body stretched to reach and her hand latched on. Each hand held the rein of the front horse. With all her strength, she tugged back as she sat astride the horse, wishing for a saddle and stirrups to brace against. Both horses slowly responded to her, which caused the others to follow suit.

"Whoa!"

The team slackened their stride. Finally they came to a halt. Lydia caught her breath and patted the shoulder of the horse. "Good boy."

As the passengers disembarked, she slid from the sweating animal. Swiftly, she unbound her skirts and flapped them into place. Shaking fingers searched the mass of tangles on her head. Combs and pins were long gone. Her hair wouldn't be as easily set to rights.

A handsome man who tried to engage her into conversation on the trip, handed her hat to her. "I snagged this for you." His brown eyes crinkled at the corners.

"Thank you." She nodded and clasped the petite hat.

"Impressive." He dipped his head and touched his wide-brimmed hat that covered sandy hair. "I would have given you a hand but I didn't fit through the window."

She assessed his broad shoulders and muscled arms. *Quite*. He wore a vest under a dark brown short waist suit coat displaying wide lapels. Cowboy boots and a gun belt strapped to his hip completed his rugged look. A slight beard covered his jaw which she considered appealing.

Passengers surrounded her as the gentleman

went back to the coach. An older woman said, "Young lady, that was very daring of you! I congratulate you for being in one piece!"

A jovial, rotund man said, "Why didn't you climb out the door?"

"Because, I tried that once and the door came off its hinges and we both landed on the ground and skidded to a stop. Running to catch up proved impossible." Lydia shrugged.

The woman looked askance and turned away muttering, "I shall never ride with her again if this is a habit of hers!" She wandered over to where the handsome gentleman surveyed the driver's wound.

"Ha! Great joke. I am still impressed. You proved a fine horsewoman." The jovial man tipped his hat and left her side.

Lydia, hat in hand, shaded her eyes against the blazing sun and scanned the horizon. If only that were a joke. Why was this becoming a habit? The shot came from somewhere and she hoped they weren't targets out in the open. Sunbeams reflected off of something metal. She hurried to the others. "We need to stay on this side of the coach. I think our assailant is still out there."

"Why do you say that?" asked the handsome man.

"I saw a reflection off metal and we're in the middle of nowhere." She nodded to the driver. "Will he be all right?"

"He will live but can't drive. He lost a lot of blood and has a nasty gash on his head. I'll take the reins unless you would like to and I can ride next to you with the coach gun. I assume you are acquainted with driving given the means you used to stop the team."

She surveyed the rest of the passengers. "I'll drive."

He helped the driver into the coach. Lydia reached in and retrieved her reticule. After the others were seated, he closed the door. She returned to the driver's seat, placed her hat atop her head, and picked up the reins as he climbed up next to her. She nodded at the shotgun. "Do you know how to use that?"

"I think I can manage." He held his lips to the side of his mouth in what she thought of a smirk. "Since we will be riding up here together, we should know each other's names. My name is Josiah Chandler." He tipped his hat.

"Lydia Blaise. Shall we get going?" She clicked her tongue against her teeth and cheek, and flicked the reins. "Giddy up!"

Josiah observed the strong hands holding the reins with skill. The lace gloves would no doubt need to be discarded. Probably ruined. Her long black hair, almost blue in hue, floated uninhibited down to her waist and the ridiculous small hat perched jauntily on her head created quite an image.

He had never met a woman as capable and daring. Tall, he would guess, maybe five-feet-eight, her lithe body had demonstrated agility and strength. Beautiful and bold. Josiah decided she must be about twenty, placing her a decade younger than he. Why had that crossed his mind?

Josiah should have been the one to jump into action. Before he could react, she'd crawled out the window. When her feet slipped, his heart had almost stopped. The dainty ankle flying through the air brought chills to the back of his neck. He wanted to jerk her back into the protection of the coach, but instead he firmly held on to her until she had her balance.

Watching her progress was excruciating as well as humorous. He would never forget the woman with her skirt up riding bareback in her underthings. Hair flying. A chuckle almost escaped as he thought of that picture engraved on his mind until his dying day.

Every time she catapulted herself to a horse, he held his breath until she seemed secure. She must know her way around horse flesh to command them to stop in their frenzy.

A movement out of his eye caused him to turn. A rider parallel to them. "We have company."

"I believe I mentioned we were not alone."

"Yes, you did."

"Are you going to use that?" She nodded her head at the shotgun.

"I'll not start shooting until needful. First, this isn't a rifle."

She snorted.

He ignored her. "Second, the man might not be mixed up in this. And third, I didn't see any more shells."

She nodded.

"Our destination is more to the left, closer to the mountain. They named it Pike's Peak from when men struck it rich discovering gold. The huge mountain stuck up out of the plains like a giant pinnacle to the clouds. There was a slogan in all the newspapers, 'Pike's Peak or Bust.' The participants in the gold rush were christened the Fifty-Niners."

With a slight move of her wrist the horses changed course. "How do you know so much about the mountain and location of Colorado City?"

"I read the newspapers and they make it sound exciting. Any boy dreams of striking it rich."

"Is the rider still following us?"

Josiah leaned out and looked behind. "He appears to be just out of reach, far enough away to not get shot." He wondered, not for the first time, why they were the target. This stage line wasn't one to carry bankroll or payroll. The plain tan Concord Stagecoach carried passengers and mail. No one on this coach appeared to be famous. Did it have anything to do with his new client?

Chapter 2

The man on horseback veered away when the town came into view. Lydia efficiently pulled the team up to where she assumed the drop off would be, near the livery. She jumped down and handed the reins to the man who seemed to be in charge. The words out of his mouth were, "What in blazes?"

"You will find all your answers by asking this gentleman, Mr. Chandler." Lydia pointed. "If you'll excuse me."

She sashayed by him as she heard Josiah Chandler hop to the ground and the door to the coach open.

Her cousin's husband stood back watching the commotion. He met her halfway. "My dear, I see you got my telegram. I'm terribly sorry I couldn't meet you in Denver as prearranged." He kissed her cheek.

"Albert, you appear in good health. I hope nothing is wrong. Your telegram didn't say. Is Edith all right?"

"Yes, yes. Fine. Which bag is yours? James will retrieve it."

She pointed to a large Jenny Lind trunk and floral wool carpetbag. A man she assumed to be James stepped forward, set her bag on top of the trunk, hefted it by the side handles and swerved off down the walkway.

"How about we enjoy a cup of tea before we head home and you can tell me why you were driving the stage." Typical steady Albert offered her his arm and led her in the other direction, to the hotel.

She glimpsed Mr. Chandler speaking to the sheriff. Lydia grinned as she passed. Mr. Chandler tipped his hat. "Ma'am."

The hotel had a nice dining room just beyond the main entrance.

Lydia said, "I'd like to freshen up a bit while you get a table."

Albert tipped his head in the direction of the facilities where she hoped a good mirror waited.

After securing her hair and washing up, she found Albert at a small round table covered with a linen cloth. The unexpected luxury surprised her in this faraway place at the edge of the plains. The room held many tables that were almost all occupied. Albert ordered tea and biscuits. Lydia surveyed the room and occupants. Her vantage point showed through the open doorway to the front of the hotel as well as passersby out the window. A good view all around.

"Edith and I are pleased you could come for a visit, and I wish to extend an invitation for you to stay as long as you would like. Edith is tickled you came all this way. She is hungry for every detail of family gossip. She told me you also keep contact with my family. We shall save that talk for around the supper table this evening as I'm well aware Edith will devour all that you say."

Their food and tea arrived. She poured for them and lathered her biscuit in butter and a red jam. He took a sip of his tea. "Now, young lady, please describe your trip."

Lydia sipped her tea and smiled. "There seemed to be someone attempting us harm. I heard a shot, the carriage jolted, and the horses sped off. Before I thought too much about it, I stopped the team." She shrugged and took a bite of her jam-covered biscuit. "Mm. This is wonderful. I've not tasted the like."

He bit into his biscuit. "Chokecherry. How in earth did you manage that from inside the coach?"

"I climbed up and proceeded to the horses. The reins were dragging the ground so I jumped upon the beasts and pulled them to a stop before more danger could befall us."

"What happened to the driver?"

"Unfortunately, he was shot and unconscious." Lydia shook her head. "Simply no help at all."

"Remarkable. I'm sure the sheriff will have some questions for you."

"I believe he is approaching."

The sheriff preceded Mr. Chandler into the room and the two men grabbed chairs and sat at their table without preamble.

Albert smirked. "Please join us. I know our competent sheriff but I'm at a disadvantage to this gentleman." He offered his hand. "Albert Miller."

"Josiah Chandler." They shook hands.

"Sheriff Hayes, may I present my wife's cousin, Miss Lydia Blaise. Lydia, Sheriff Hayes."

Lydia acknowledged with a nod.

Sheriff Hayes asked, "Miss Blaise, can you give me an account of the incident on the stagecoach?"

Lydia swiftly and briefly told the events as she had reported it to her cousin. At the end of her telling, she glanced at Mr. Chandler who seemed to be holding in a smile but didn't keep the twinkle out of his eye. She felt he might explode any moment. She quickly regarded her tea and took a sip. A chuckle out of her now wouldn't help.

Under her dark lashes she saw the sheriff scrutinize her and then Mr. Chandler. "I see. Well, all appears to be the same and yet completely different. Miss Blaise, you understate your incredible accomplishment. According to Mr. Chandler here, you performed an amazing feat. I take my hat off to you. Humble, and beautiful." He nudged Mr. Chandler in the ribs.

Her face grew hot, something she had never been able to corral. Horses, yes, but the infernal blushing had a mind of its own.

The sheriff continued, "Thank you, Miss. It's been a pleasure and I look forward to visiting with you again."

She looked up. "Sheriff, how is the driver?"

"He will be right as a gun in no time. Don't worry." He stood. "I must be off on my rounds." He picked up his hat and dipped his head. Miss. Gentlemen." With purpose he strode from the room.

Albert said, "What brings you to our fine town, Mr. Chandler?"

"Adventure. The West. Back to my roots. My parents homesteaded near here but when Pa died, Ma took me and my sister and brother to her folks in Chicago. I've been itchin' to come back to these parts for over a decade." He glanced out the window where the mountains poked above the buildings on the other side of the street. "As beautiful as I remember."

"What line of work are you in?"

"I've tried my hand at about everything but recently held a position as an estate manager and bookkeeper. I've done well with figures all my life."

"Here is my card." Albert handed Mr. Chandler a small white card. "Edith would love to meet the young man who helped our sweet Lydia. Come on out for supper. Are you staying at the hotel?"

Lydia glanced between the two men. *Why would Albert extend an invitation to this virtual stranger? Albert wouldn't try to initiate an attraction between us. Surely not. Something else is brewing.*

Mr. Chandler scanned the area. "Seems to be a busy place. The doc gave me a name of a boarding house if there aren't rooms available."

"Miss Maddie's is a fine establishment. I've been told the home cooked meals are worthy of praise. Lydia, are you finished?"

Lydia wiped her mouth on the cloth napkin and nodded. "Yes. Thank you."

Her cousin fixed his gaze on Mr. Chandler. "Seven o'clock. Head out of town to the north a piece. The directions are on the back of my card. Lydia, are you ready to start for home?"

Mr. Chandler stood. "If you will excuse me. I'll be off to find accommodations."

Lydia rose and gathered her embroidered purple silk reticule—a purchase she'd made to go with her traveling outfit, which fit her perfectly. An expense she didn't normally indulge in. She prayed she would be able to get the horse flesh and sweat smell out of the garment.

Together they made their way to the buggy where James waited to drive them to her cousin's home.

The gorgeous sunny day swirled pleasant breezes with fragrant aromas of sage and wildflowers. Lydia asked, "What are the names of these colorful blooms?"

Albert pointed out Cowboy's Delight, Columbine, blue flax, and alpine sunflowers. Scattered along the way were the familiar yellow dandelions. Beauty abounded everywhere she looked and the ever-present mountain reigned over the landscape, reaching up into the wisps of clouds and the deep blue of the sky. She sat in awe of the creation surrounding her. The clean crisp air filled her lungs and a sweet peace radiated through her.

Lydia felt herself relax after her harrowing morning.

The drive took a while. Around a bend, an expansive house appeared. Four outbuildings and a huge garden ensconced the sides. Rose bushes in staggering colors of red, pink, yellow, and white rowed the front of the wraparound covered porch. Eaves, painted in the same hue of blue as the railing, and curtained windows with open shutters of red, greeted them. The three-story stood wide and proud.

Impressed, Lydia let her eyes travel to reveal other magical beauties. A stone bird bath posed near a wooden bench under a large oak tree with a nest mostly hidden in a high branch. Farther back, in another tree, she spied a swing swaying in the breeze. A rabbit ran across the lawn.

Idyllic. Her cousin Edith had put her decorating skills to work. Lydia couldn't wait until she stepped into the house. The buggy came to a stop in front of the steps to the porch. The door opened. There she was, her sweet cousin, Edith. Lydia didn't wait to be helped down but scooted out and rushed to an anticipated embrace. The women wept with joy.

The hotel was fully booked so Josiah picked his way to Miss Maddie's boarding house, to be served tea fit for a king. A kind, old-ish lady—Miss Maddie. She ran a proper house and so far proved a wonderful cook with her warm flaky biscuits and berry jam.

Josiah washed up and changed into a nicer suit than the one he had traveled in. He asked Miss Maddie to brush his traveling suit and wash the shirt, cuffs, and collar. He had been in the clothes for too many days. She guaranteed them to recover and not to worry.

Earlier, before heading over to the boarding house, Josiah acquired a horse. The livery had a grey mare for him to rent for the duration of his stay. His assignment seemed to be developing nicely. He hoped he might transfer soon into the residence of his client. That prospect had more perks than he currently wanted to think about.

Instead, he strapped his pistol to the small of his back and checked his other weapons—a knife and derringer concealed under his pant leg. He took precautions and slipped a thread between the door and jam. He needed to be aware if anyone snooped into his room while he was out.

Downstairs, he poked his head in the sitting room and found the mistress of the establishment dusting the fireplace mantle. "Miss Maddie, I'll be back in a few hours. Thank you for tending to my duds. I'll grab them tomorrow—no need to climb the stairs." He donned his hat, mounted the mare, and headed to the Miller's home.

He had memorized the instructions and arrived in the half hour he had given himself.

The house welcomed him with a hitching post for his horse and an inviting porch with the front door painted a cheery blue standing wide open. He bounded up the three steps and knocked on the frame.

A man in a suit answered. "You must be Mr. Chandler. I'm Horace. Master Miller is expecting you in his study. I'll take your hat if you don't mind."

Josiah handed him his hat.

"Right this way, sir."

Josiah had heard many accents and guessed him to be proper English. He followed through the long hall flanked by rooms on each side. He glimpsed a fully equipped and decorated sitting room, dining room, and a room with a piano. The impressive hall had portraits on the walls and skinny tables with ornamentation. Unbelievably, a suit of armor stood in the corner fully decked out with helmet, mace, and sword. They passed two closed doors before they approached another.

Horace knocked softly.

"Enter," came the response from inside.

Horace preceded Josiah. "Mr. Chandler arrived, sir."

"Thank you, Horace. Please see that Edith is aware." Sitting behind a massive desk, Mr. Miller motioned for Josiah to enter. "Come in and take a seat. Care for a smoke?" A curl of vapor floated up from the pipe between his teeth.

The room was lined with shelves filled with books. Behind the desk hung a massive landscape—the formidable snowcapped Pike's Peak with a small town mapped out at the basin.

Josiah took the proffered chair. "No thank you. But please." He waved his host to continue with his pipe.

"Nuisance, these." He wiggled the smoking pipe in his hand. "Ah, but a welcome one. Thank you for accepting my invitation. Now, let me assure you we can talk in privacy here."

"I would prefer the outdoors where ears can't be hidden." He stood and gestured toward the double doors. Shall we?"

"All right, I'll humor you."

Josiah led them into the field behind the house he had observed when he arrived. "Now, what were you going to say?"

"You are aware, today I should have been on the stage. Unfortunately we had a birthing, a calf about rip the mama apart getting out. No way could I go. Thank the good Lord you and Lydia were not injured. I am relieved the driver was only winged. I wouldn't want that on my conscience. What do you think would have happened had I been on the stage?"

"The ramifications are appalling. Probably tried to finish the job and got rid of witnesses to boot. As it lies, Lydia saved the day and when everyone got off the coach the perpetrator saw you weren't aboard. That cousin of yours is amazing. Never in my life have I seen a gal do anything as daring. What a sight with her skirt tucked up and, in her underthings, leap onto frightened horses."

Mr. Miller grinned. "You paint a picture she might want you to forget. She downplayed her part for sure. I could tell by the sheriff and your faces, there was more to the story. She jumped onto the horse?"

"And continued to the lead horses and slowed them from there. I tried to view her movements from inside the coach and kept lookout for more trouble. At the start, I thought the best place for me would be to ride up with the driver. He objected and since I had no real cause, I agreed to sit with the passengers."

"Don't you carry a badge or something to show?"

"I understood you wanted this kept secret? Anyway, I'm a detective not a marshal. I only investigate and call the sheriff when there is enough evidence for an arrest. Now, is anyone else aware of our arrangement?"

"No. We will keep referring to you as someone I met and enjoy keeping company. If that isn't convincing, I'll hire you to audit my books or something. Who knows, my manager may need help? He'd be hell fired mad but I think I could calm him. Edith, my wife, is not privy. She mentioned getting the sheriff to call in the marshals to investigate but I want this all under wraps."

"Any more problems since the dog's poisoning and the jimmying of your hunting rifle?"

"Nothing, except for a watcher I glimpsed in the wee hours. Seemed strange to glimpse a silhouette near those trees up the hill." He motioned toward a stand of poplars. "Golden, who almost died from poison, had her hackles standing, and a low growl rumbled in her throat. I tell you she gave me goose flesh on my arms. I spied the shadow and believed the killer awaited. I haven't slept much since and have gone to taking James with me everywhere. He's good with a firearm and has a worthy head on his shoulders." Mr. Miller held up his hand. "Before you say anything, I told him my shoulder is giving me trouble and needed him to drive."

Josiah's jaw tightened. *Someone is persistent. Albert won't be harmed on my watch. I'll stick like glue to the gentleman. Long tedious nights are in the near future before I can catch the culprit. At this point everyone I meet is suspect. Except of course, the beautiful Miss Blaise.* "All right. You can sleep well tonight, I will be on guard duty."

"In a day or so, I will ease you closer to the family and ask you to stay with us. Move your things here to make your constant presence appear natural and easy."

"I believe your wife is looking for you."

Mr. Miller turned to see his wife through the window. "We better go in."

Josiah followed him into the house. Mr. Miller kissed his wife's cheek. "Dear, I'd like for you to meet the young man Lydia met on the stage today, Josiah Chandler. Mr. Chandler, my lovely wife, Edith Miller."

Josiah received her small delicate hand, bowed, and briefly kissed her fingers. "Ma'am. A pleasure."

"A gentleman. Gracious me. No one has greeted me in that fashion since coming out West." She turned. "Lydia dear, Mr. Chandler has come with his charm and good manners."

Lydia approached and he clasped her proffered fingers and kissed her hand, lingering a fraction longer than necessary. She smelled heavenly of rose and honey. A heady aroma. He needed to be careful. She wasn't part of the job. Moving in would make this an interesting arrangement and avoidance quite difficult. A thrill he concealed made his heart beat a bit faster.

"Come, supper is ready to be served." Mrs. Miller took her husband's arm and moved toward the dining room he had seen earlier.

There was nothing to be done but offer his arm to the dark haired beauty beside him. Not an unpleasant occupation. Her cool fingers rested lightly on his arm. He would be proud to escort her anytime. Lovely women had been on his arm on many occasions. Part of the job. Physical attraction was not new. Dozens of women had crossed his path and a few had turned into a relationship of differing degrees. Someday, might one engage his mind as well as his heart?

Lydia's senses reacted to the handsome and charming man seated across the table from her. Sophisticated and educated with a touch of ruggedness, Josiah appealed to her womanly sensitivities. She fell under his spell when he spoke, and extremely so when his eyes caught hers. Dangerous. She didn't want a man's attention, yet she responded.

Levi, Edith and Albert's son, and his wife Susanna arrived for supper. The last time she had seen him, they had been children. His beautiful wife, though uppity, sat next to Lydia across from Levi. Men on one side and women on the other with Albert and Edith on opposite ends.

She had a hard time concentrating on the conversation. Her mind questioned, what was wrong with her? To clear her thoughts, she let her eyes trail around the room and placed the pieces of furnishings in the era of their craftsmanship.

The Sheraton period sideboard was more functional than ornamental. The large table and chairs with elaborate carving she perceived as Victorian style. The paraffin lamps were more delicate and added a bit of elegance along with the green and gold brocade draperies across the windows. The wool rugs she guessed were from abroad. Amazing décor for an out-of-way place in the Colorado Territory, to be sure. Her cousin must have spent a small fortune and many years to acquire everything. Edith's sense of artistic flair hadn't diminished.

"Lydia dear, what is in your pretty head?"

Lydia jerked and almost spilled her tea. "I'm sorry, Cousin. I was admiring your beautiful furnishings. You did a marvelous job. You were saying?"

Edith laughed. "Mr. Chandler declined a smoke with Levi and my husband. Albert suggested you two catch some air. Why don't you take him out to visit the new calf? Susanna and I need to discuss a few things about the upcoming birth."

Lydia had suspected Susanna to be with child. She had eaten mostly apples. Strange when at her fingertips sat other tasty dishes. Lydia placed her napkin next to her plate. "I'd be delighted. Shall we?"

Lydia allowed Josiah to help her with her shawl. Normally she donned her shawl or coat without allowing help. Edith wouldn't approve of Lydia's independence even though she had crossed the thousands of miles by herself. Lydia complied only to appease her hostess.

She led the way to the barn that housed the calf. On the tour of the grounds earlier, she had been told the birth had been traumatic and they wanted to keep an eye on the baby for a day or so. She didn't understand why they coddled the calf but this gave her an excuse to experience first-hand farm life up close. She was an expert horsewoman, but never spent much time around livestock.

The calf's large brown eyes met hers and she fell in love. Lashes so long and delicate outlined the sad eyes. "She is beautiful, do you agree?"

"Yes she is."

She swiveled her head and realized he didn't

look at the calf but her. She turned to avoid him noticing her blush. She went into the pen to pet the calf. The fur was stiffer than a horse. The tied-up mom stood in the corner, munching on hay. The cow appeared to be fine after her ordeal.

After composing herself she returned to his side of the gate. "Do you plan on a lengthy stay in Colorado City?"

"Depends on a few things. I'm enjoying my time so far. How long will you be here?"

"My parents passed away and Cousin Edith asked me to come. Plans are indefinite."

"I'm sorry. I didn't realize. You don't carry sorrow. You seem happy, joyful."

She smiled. "Thank you. I miss them but I can't bring them back. They wouldn't want me to 'carry sorrow,' as you put it. Anyway, why wallow in self-pity?"

"That's an incredible way to look at a tragedy."

"I don't want to be coddled like this calf. If they were wild animals, they would be outside and free not in this warm building out of the elements. The calf and momma will eventually brave the world. Why not at birth?"

He scanned the calf and the mother. "Yes. I see what you mean."

"Edith may have something to do with this. She is a kind-hearted soul."

They went back into the house to enjoy fresh apple pie with the others. Levi and Susanna were staying the night. Levi said, "My wife finds the jostle on the wagon a bit harrowing and so we make the trip once a week and stay a few days."

Soon, Josiah donned his hat and Horace let him out the front door where his horse waited, tied to the hitching post.

Lydia climbed the stairs to her room. Upon entering, she turned down her lamp the maid had lit for her. The windows overlooked the garden and she had a good view of the bench and bird bath. She sat near the window to gaze into the dark and listen to the quiet. Brush in hand, stroking her tresses, she thought about the family, their visitor, and the events of the day. Brushing her hair always relaxed her at the end of the day.

Shattering glass broke the stillness of the night.

She bolted upright in her chair, coming out of her sleepiness.

A scream!

Author Photo: Jamie Herrera Photography
https://www.jamieherreraphotography.com/

Robin and her husband Jimmy are in the process of relocating to the Nashville area of Tennessee. Together, they celebrate with seventeen grandchildren. An award winner for romance and flash fiction, Robin is multi-published and writes stories on her blog for children. Robin is a member of ACFW, Vice President of ACFW Colorado Western Slope, and member of John316 Marketing Network. She enjoys leading a Bible study group and singing in two community choirs. Robin loves company and challenging her young guests to discover the many giraffes in the obvious and hidden nooks and crannies of their home.

Visit her at:

Blog, Robin Densmore Fuson
http://www.robindensmorefuson.com/
Blog, kid Bible lessons
http://www.kidbiblelessons.com/
Amazon author page
https://www.amazon.com/Robin-Densmore-Fuson/e/B06XGKVDDV/ref
Twitter, https://twitter.com/RobinLFuson
Facebook, https://www.facebook.com/AuthorRobinDensmoreFuson/
Google+
https://plus.google.com/u/0/+RobinDensmoreFuson
Pinterest
https://www.pinterest.com/revelation411/reflection-in-glass/
Goodreads
https://www.goodreads.com/author/show/6604786.Robin_Densmore_Fuson
Instagram
https://www.instagram.com/robindensmorefuson/

Made in the USA
Monee, IL
05 March 2020